A Rough Crowd

The pillory, a wooden contraption ... connected by a hinge, resembled a pair of jaws. It was designed to clamp over a person's neck and wrists and hold him immobile, both to facilitate further punishment and to permit the assembled townspeople to stare at him.

Daniel Willard trembled uncontrollably as the sheriff drew Daniel's hands into the pillory. The sheriff closed the top plank and shot the locking bolt home with a loud clank. Daniel cast his eyes about at the crowd. He couldn't raise his head enough to see anyone's face, nor could he lower his head enough to hide his own, so he gazed at the crowd at waist level, his eyes clouding with tears.

The sheriff carefully flattened Daniel's ear against the wood of the pillory, then held an iron house nail against it, taking careful aim with a hammer.

At the back of the crowd, seventeen-year-old Mindy Gold looked on, both repelled and fascinated. *How far are these people going to take this Puritan reenactment,* she asked herself.

With a loud thunk, the hammer fell. The nail sunk into Daniel's ear, pinning it to the wood of the pillory. Daniel screamed, and a jet of his blood sprayed out, flecking the crowd.

Mindy's eyes widened in horror. Who were these people? And how on Earth was she going to get out of there?

All titles in the **Smart Novels** series:

SAT Vocabulary

Busted

Head Over Heels

Sun-Kissed

Vampire Dreams

Rave New World

S.C.A.M.

U.S. History

Volume I: A Time for Witches

Volume II: Shades of Blue and Gray

Volume III: Reckless Revolution

Volume IV: Gilded Delirium

smart novels
U.S. HISTORY

A Time for Witches

Volume I

by Lynne Hansen

Spark Publishing
A Division of Barnes & Noble
120 Fifth Avenue
New York, NY 10011
www.sparknotes.com

ISBN-13: 978-1-4114-9671-2
ISBN-10: 1-4114-9671-X

Library of Congress Cataloging-in-Publication Data

Hansen, Lynne, 1968–
    A time for witches / by Lynne Hansen.
        p. cm.—(Smart Novels)
    Summary: Growing up in Salem, Massachusetts, seventeen-year-old Mindy Gold learned much about the town's famous witch trials but when a strange man takes her back in time to colonial Salem, her ignorance threatens to make her the next victim of hysteria.
    ISBN-13: 978-1-4114-9671-2
    ISBN-10: 1-4114-9671-X
    [1. Time travel—Fiction. 2. Trials (Witchcraft)—Fiction. 3. Extraterrestrial beings—Fiction. 4. Salem (Mass.)—History—Colonial period, ca. 1600-1775—Fiction. 5. Science fiction.] I. Title.
    PZ7.H198252Tim 2007
    [Fic]—dc22

                                                                2007019347

Please submit changes or report errors to www.sparknotes.com/errors.

Printed and bound in the United States.

10 9 8 7 6 5 4 3 2 1

CONTENTS

FROM THE CHRONOLYZER'S HARD DRIVE:

Chapter One

Present-Day Salem, Massachusetts; Halloween night

"I need you to bring me twenty bucks and my pepper spray key chain by midnight," Mindy Gold's younger sister Serena said, her voice crackling over the poor connection.

Mindy held the cell phone to her ear with her shoulder and pulled her thick, curly brown hair up in a neon pink scrunchy. "Where are you? The connection's garbage."

"Pioneer Village."

"Isn't that closed for renovations?" Mindy knew that Serena had been gallivanting about at some Halloween living-history museum all day, but she'd sort of tuned out whenever Serena went into details.

"You never listen to a thing I say, do you? They've finished a bunch of the renovations, but they opened up special for Salem's Haunted Happenings."

"For the tourists, you mean."

In modern-day Salem, life always seemed to revolve around tourism. A million visitors flocked to the city every year to buy into its major industry: witchcraft-themed kitsch. Witch-shaped cookie-cutters, seventy-dollar witch Christmas ornaments—you name it, and it could be found for sale at one of the local gift shops. But the city's tendency to revel in its own past went far beyond shops and gifts. From the statue of *Bewitched* star Elizabeth Montgomery in the town square to the witch logos on the police cars and high school football team uniforms, the city of Salem would never let you forget what it was famous for.

Seventeen-year-old Mindy refused to buy into it. Every October, in every grade since elementary school, she had learned all about the witch trials. She had spent her time thinking about the events of 1692, decided that they were horrifying and depressing, and moved on. She thought the whole history-kitsch industry was just unseemly— a bald-faced attempt to make money off of a tragedy.

Mindy didn't consider the historical reenactors who worked in the area to be much better than the shopkeepers. As far as she was concerned, playing a prim, big-rumped Puritan wasn't any different than playing a witch or psychic to extort money from fanny-packed tourists looking for black and orange "Witches Know How To Spell" T-shirts. But her sister Serena was, as usual, a different story. Serena was fanatical about historical reenactment. She claimed it was far more real and legitimate than any history lesson in books and spent whatever cash she could wring from their mother on materials for authentic colonial-era costumes. This hobby had come about through the influence of Serena's relatively new best friend, Irene, who had been doing historical reenactments throughout New England since she was ten. Irene's parents homeschooled her so that she could pursue her interests—wherever they led. But as far as Mindy was concerned, Irene had a lot to answer for.

Serena sighed. "So are you going to bring me my money or not?"

"Why do you need pepper spray?"

"You know those homeless punk rockers who hang around the bus station collecting change with that one-eared dog? I think they're here at Pioneer Village."

"So? I thought they were pretty harmless. Aren't they like, anarchists or something?"

"Yeah, I know, and actually it's just one of them. This guy with a Mohawk and a black leather coat. He's just . . . he seems *wasted* or something. He keeps going from booth to booth, chuckling and making inappropriate comments."

"Like what?" Mindy asked, trying not to sound worried.

"Just stupid stuff—like if we were real Puritans we wouldn't be wearing underwear."

"Isn't there a security guard or something?"

"It's not a big deal. I'd just like to have the pepper spray in case the perv decides we *are* real Puritans." Serena forced a laugh, but Mindy heard tenseness in her voice.

"I'm going to come get you," Mindy said.

"Stop trying to act like Mom and just bring me my money. There's this fabulous Celtic knot necklace I've just got to have, and Mistress Rhianna said she'd only hold it for me until midnight."

When Serena went into her stop-trying-to-be-Mom mode, there was no way she'd take any kind of advice or instruction from Mindy. It wasn't Mindy's fault. Their parents had divorced five years ago when Mindy was twelve, and Mom had put Mindy in charge. Serena hated being told what to do by someone who was only two years older than she was just as much as Mindy hated having to always be the responsible one. Serena was even more difficult now that they were both attending Salem High School.

"*Hello,*" Serena said exasperatedly. "Money. Bring it to me."

"Where is it?"

"Not until you promise you're going to bring it to me."

"Do you know how much money you already owe Mom and me

for all that costume stuff you buy? I should ransack your room right now and put that twenty bucks toward what you owe us."

"You'll never find it, and if you go into my room without permission, I'll tell Mom."

Mindy shoved her hands into the pockets of her hoodie. "Fine."

"Promise you'll bring it to me."

"I promise. Now where is it?"

"It's underneath the sole of my white Keds."

"You don't have any white Keds."

"Sure I do. They're the ones I drew the hearts on."

"Those are gray."

"They used to be white."

"Ew. How about I just bring the shoe, and you dig around for the twenty?"

"Fine by me, but there's one more thing."

"What?"

"You'll have to wear one of my costumes to get in."

"Yeah, right."

"We've hit the max number of people the fire department will allow in, so you'll have to say you're here to relieve one of the actors."

"You're joking. I'm not getting dressed up in *garb* just to bring you money. Meet me in the parking lot in a half hour."

"I can't. My break's just about over, and I'm playing one of the accused witches in the next scene. It's a big part. I can't just skip out."

"Not even for a fabulous Celtic knot necklace?"

"No. Look, I've got to go. I'm working the Governor's House. It's the first one on the left. I've gotta go."

The phone went dead.

Mindy tossed her head, her scrunchy-bound ponytail bobbing. She pulled it tighter. If it were just the money, Serena could go without her stupid necklace, but this drugged-out homeless guy worried her. It was high season at the gift shop, and Mom was working late. So the only way to make sure Serena made it home safely was to go to Pioneer Village and hang out until Serena was done for the night. Being the big sister sucked.

After locating the twenty-dollar bill and spending far too long trying to figure out which layer of wool petticoat and waistcoat went over which other layer, Mindy finally headed for Pioneer Village.

Located on the south side of Salem in the corner of an eleven-acre park surrounded by Salem Harbor on one side and a green chain-link fence on the others, Pioneer Village was something people usually drove right past. Not on Halloween, though. Tonight the little league ballpark just outside the village teemed with self-proclaimed witches and psychics, as well as row after row of vendors selling everything from pewter jewelry to wooden geese sporting jaunty witch hats.

At eleven-thirty, Mindy parked her ancient hatchback beneath a black and orange vinyl banner that proclaimed, "Welcome to Pioneer Village's Haunted Happenings Celebration! Come and Stay a Spell!"

Mindy groaned at the corny sign. *Too typical,* she thought.

She had to suck in her gut as she got out of the hatchback so that she wouldn't bust a button. At fifteen, Serena hadn't developed the waist and curves Mindy had, and the olive outfit pulled Mindy in relentlessly—and not in a good way. Luckily the Puritan version of the costume came with a square white linen collar that covered anything that might be likely to pop out awkwardly.

The tourists waiting in line to get in gawked at Mindy as she approached the ticket booth. Her scalp prickled, and she felt the heat rise in her cheeks. Boy, she hoped she didn't know any of these people. She'd just die if someone recognized her dressed like a renaissance fair freak. She just wanted to get in, get her sister, and leave.

"I need to get in, please," she said to the skinny, black-haired boy working the booth. She didn't recognize him from school, but he looked to be about her age. He had piercing emerald eyes and wore a faded black Ministry concert T-shirt.

"Full up," he said, jutting a pale, skinny finger toward the line of anxious tourists. "Wait there. Three people leave, three people enter." He looked back down at the magazine he was reading.

Mindy scanned the line. There were probably a hundred people waiting to go in. She'd never get inside by midnight, much less find her sister by then. She'd come all this way for nothing. It couldn't get any worse.

And then it did.

A cool, sexy guy's voice called to her. "Mindy? Mindy Gold? Is that you?"

Cast of Characters:

The 9 Types of Salem Villager

How on Earth did witch-hunting hysteria come to engulf the little town of Salem? Theories abound, but considering the cast of characters involved, a bloodthirsty witch hunt seems like a pretty obvious outcome.

Irate Farmers

Seventeenth-century Salem farmers were just like farmers anywhere during any other time period, with one key difference: They couldn't actually grow anything. New England soil is some of the rockiest in America. It's entirely unfit for raising anything edible, except for maybe cranberries, which grow in bogs, not fields. So what's a Puritan farmer to do? Many tried to acquire as much land as possible to maximize potentially farmable acreage. Eventually, though, the land ran out, and farmers started bumping into each other's plots. Farms stopped growing, and fences went up. And you know how neighbors can get—one guy complains because the neighbor's kids aren't pious enough, while another lusts after the goodwife next door. Pretty soon everyone's up in arms and just itchin' for the chance to stab each other in the back.

Even More Irate Farmers

As if neighborly rivalry wasn't enough, farmers within the same family were often at each other's throats. As land became more scarce, each generation of farmer-fathers had less land to bequeath to their farmer-sons. And when you have five or six sons, you have a big problem on your hands. Farms eventually became so small that only the eldest son got the booty, while the younger ones simply got the boot. Many of those ousted younger sons went into business as fishermen, merchants, and traders. No wonder New England eventually created the most vibrant industrial economy in the New World, ultimately allowing them to kick the South's butt in the Civil War. It all goes back to those land-pinched Puritans.

Goodwives

A goodwife in colonial New England was the original all-American stay-at-home soccer mom. She cooked, she cleaned, she baked, and she did it all without so much as a smile on her pious lips. She dressed very modestly, wore no jewelry or makeup, said her prayers daily, and made sure her family did too. She also gardened and worked day and night with her hands as the family tailor and seamstress. Sound too good to be true? Probably was, but many colonial woman aspired to this brand of perfection. In reality, most women probably bent some of the rules now and then like the desperate goodwives they undoubtedly were.

Badwives

Then there were the women who threw caution to the wind and said to hell with being a goody-two-shoes goodwife. These were the women who bucked convention and didn't really care about putting on a good front. These were feminists before the word *feminist* had even been invented. Many of these ladies had husbands, of course, but they challenged traditional English gender norms by doing "men's" work, such as selling stuff for profit (gasp!) or engaging in small real estate or other business transactions (horrors!). Some townsfolk didn't take kindly to such flagrant disregard for the way things had always been done, which is why so many of these women found themselves accused of witchcraft.

Trying Teenage Girls

Salem teenagers were no doubt bored witless. What did they have to do? They could milk cows, do chores, or pray. Or they could daydream about growing up, having seven or eight babies—and milking cows, doing chores, and praying. And you thought you had it bad with your iPod, cell phone, and 500 TV channels. With nothing to do and all those hormones raging, these girls were just ripe for a good old-fashioned witch hunt.

Pious Preachers

According to the Puritan faith, God had determined which people would be saved before they'd even been born, and actions performed on Earth had nothing to do with one's fate. But that didn't stop Puritan preachers from seeing sorcery in the most insignificant events. Guy got lucky and had a bountiful harvest? Witch! Goodwife could read and write her own name? Witch! Kid grew taller as she got older? Witch!

Alcoholic Toddlers

Contrary to popular belief, Puritans were regular lushes. All of 'em: men, women, guys, gals, toddlers, even the dogs. Okay, maybe not the dogs, but you get the idea. The colonists drank beer, cider, rum, wine, ale, and harder stuff 24/7. They imbibed so frequently in part because alcohol was safer than the bacteria-infested water. But kicking back with a cold one was one of the few pleasures of colonial life. So why do we associate teatotaling with the Puritans? Well, Puritans frowned on drunkenness, of course, but New

England manufacturers in the nineteenth century were the ones who really insisted on abstinence. A piss-drunk Puritan farmer stumbling around his fields never hurt anyone, but a wasted factory hand could do some serious damage. And voila, a myth was born.

Native Americans

Yep, they were there too, although the Puritans tried their damnedest to pretend they didn't exist. The Native Americans had shown the Puritans how to plant and grow corn, and what did they get in return? Smallpox. The Native Americans had helped the Puritans survive their first winter, and what did they get in return? Their lands taken. The Native Americans had even broken bread with the Puritans, as legend would have it, at the first Thanksgiving. And all for what? To be shunned and forced to convert (even though no one really believed they'd be saved).

Quaker Outcasts

Think everyone in colonial New England was a Puritan? Think again. Although most people did belong to the Puritan Church, not everyone was happy with the status quo. In an irony of ironies, the Puritans left Europe in search of a place where they could practice their faith freely, but they refused that same privilege to any Puritans in their midst who had their own ideas about God. Like most hypocrites, the Puritans could dish it out, but they couldn't take it. They banished the dissenters, who in turn often founded their own townships and colonies. When a significant minority of people got tired of being told how to live, they either formed their own churches or signed up with another faith, such as the Quakers. The Quakers believed in some newfangled, funky ideas, such as making peace rather than war and extending basic rights to women.

Chapter Two

Mindy wanted to pull her white linen cap down until it covered her whole face. Instead, she turned and mumbled, "Uh, hi, Chad."

"Dude! Did you get bit by the history bug like your sister?" a tall, handsome skater boy with shoulder-length wavy blond hair and cat-like green eyes asked.

"Not really."

Mindy and Chad Pembrooke had known each other since pre-school, when they shared their first kiss in a refrigerator box they'd turned into a pet hospital. Four-year-old Mindy hadn't appreciated it one bit and had punched him and made him eat a green crayon. She'd regretted it ever since, swearing to herself that if Chad ever kissed her again, it would not result in forced crayon consumption.

The summer before sixth grade, Chad's parents took him to Europe for vacation. He came back right before middle school started, and Mindy had been floored. In three months he'd grown several inches, learned to skateboard and speak French, and basically turned into a big old slice of cool—a coolslice who had girls drooling all over him and who seemed to want to have nothing to do with Mindy.

Behind Chad, his girlfriend, Veronica Stevens, sighed and cocked her head, her blond ringlets quivering with amusement. "You auditioning for *America's Next Top Model,* Gold?" She stepped forward and wrapped her willowy arm around Chad's trim bicep.

Chad leaned over and kissed Veronica lightly on the lips. "She's okay, Ronnie. If Mindy's got guts enough to go in, maybe we should try it."

Veronica pouted out her lower lip. "But I'm not done shopping."

"I don't even know what's inside," Mindy said, desperate not to be the reason the hottest couple at Salem High plunked down cash to go see some lame living history exhibit. "I'm just here for my sister."

The ticket booth guy looked up at her, bored. "Your sister's one of the actors?"

Mindy nodded. "Yeah." She held her breath but didn't make eye contact.

"Go ahead in," he finally said, then looked back at his magazine.

Mindy scuttled through the gate.

"Bye, Mindy," Chad called after her. "Maybe we'll see you inside."

Waving half-heartedly, Mindy slipped into the welcoming dimness of the wood-lined path. That's all she needed—Chad Pembrooke and his cheerleader Barbie doll following her around in this stupid getup just to laugh at her.

Mindy stumbled over the hem of one of the petticoats. Serena was going to be so dead when Mindy finally found her.

Off to the right, a pond stretched sullenly into the dark. On the left, about a hundred feet down the dirt path, tourists thronged around a weathered, two-story clapboard building with diamond-paned windows.

And just apart from the crowd was the black-leather-clad punk rocker her sister had told her about. He had a dazed look on his face, and even though the evening air was cool, he was sweating. Mindy was struck by how young he looked and how unthreatening he seemed. He had the look of a stray puppy dog about him—and

Mindy could never resist strays. She walked up to him and caught his eye.

"You don't look too well. Are you all right?"

"Oh, it's you again," he mumbled.

Mindy blinked. The young man nodded in recognition, looking like he was in pain and didn't much care whether Mindy talked to him or not. Sitting on the ground, he had his arms wrapped around himself tightly, his hands tucked under his armpits. Sweat poured down his face. He looked up at her irritably and said, "I seem to remember we shared a past together recently."

Mindy paused. She knew she'd never seen this guy at the bus stop, under a bridge, or anywhere else. It was clear he was mentally ill or perhaps just on drugs. Still, he was so obviously suffering that Mindy was more sorry for him than afraid of him. A slight, skinny teenager wearing a coat two sizes too big for him, he didn't seem like a particularly intimidating specimen.

"No, no," Mindy said placatingly. "You must be thinking of one of your other, uh, friends."

The boy shot her a baleful look and shrugged. "Whatever. Past, present, and future just confuse me. Can we not talk about this?" The sweat was now dripping off him like water from a soaked rag.

"Listen, what's wrong with you? Can I help you?" Mindy's voice was gentle yet urgent.

"I just need my . . . *medicine*."

Mindy rolled her eyes and sighed. She had a good idea what his "medicine" was, and she definitely didn't want him taking it in public near children, where her own sister worked. The boy spoke again.

"Don't even talk to me about mercy." He leaned over in pain, shaking his head. "I don't even want to discuss mercy."

"Look, you need to get out of here," Mindy told him. "You're going to get in trouble if you stay here. I don't think you can get what you're looking for here." *At least, I sure hope not*, she thought.

The boy looked up at her pleadingly. "They're already after me. That guy in the costume is a *narc*." He spat the word out. "A real dredger, you know? I just want to find a way out of this place, out of this . . . this *body*."

"There's a rear exit over there between those two buildings," Mindy pointed. "Why don't you go and lie down. At least until you're feeling better."

The boy shrugged and nodded, looking very much like he wanted to throw up. "Don't tell that guy where I am. Please," he added.

"Look, I won't, okay? Just go." Mindy tried not to sound impatient.

The young man in the black coat shuffled off quickly, as Mindy turned toward the Governor's House in search of her sister. As she approached, the crowd broke into spontaneous applause.

Mindy checked her square white collar. Nothing was poking out. She checked her uncomfortable leather shoes. No toilet paper trailing behind. Why were they clapping?

The crowd filtered apart. A seven-year-old girl, pulling her reluctant father behind her, ran up to Mindy. "Here's one of the actors now!" the girl squealed, her pigtails bobbing. "Oh, Daddy! Can you take my picture with her?"

The man shrugged and held up his camera. "Do you mind?"

Mindy shook her head. Easier to just go along with it than try to explain why she was dressed up like this if she wasn't an actress. She knelt next to the seven-year-old and smiled perfunctorily. The father snapped the picture and plodded after his daughter, already on the trail of another living-history "celebrity."

Standing up and flicking a leaf from the hem of her petticoat, Mindy noticed a handsome young man in costume leaning against an elm tree watching her. He was very small and delicate-looking—no bigger than Mindy herself—and wore a drab black suit that made him look like he'd walked out of a painting of the first Thanksgiving. Beneath his cloak and squared-off white linen collar, he wore a fitted jacket; baggy, knee-length breeches; knit stockings with garters tied to hold them up; and clunky square leather shoes. A tall, rounded felt hat pressed his curly brown hair onto his forehead. He leaned forward inquiringly.

"Sure and I don't remember seeing you in that last scene," he said with a playful lilt in his voice, his hazel eyes sparkling mischievously. His face, with its sharp, high cheekbones and smooth, pale skin was almost preternaturally beautiful. It was a face that would have seemed more appropriate on a young woman, but his voice, with its rich Irish brogue, was unmistakably masculine.

Mindy blushed. "I didn't mean to act like I was an actor—I mean, that little girl just thought I was a reenactor and I—" Mindy's shoulders dropped as she lapsed into silence, tongue-tied.

"Ah, never ye mind," the young man said with a wink. "I won't be telling anyone. Besides, I don't think impersonating an actor impersonating a Congregationalist is a crime—at least, not in the twenty-first century."

"Congregationalist?"

"Sure and that's what the Puritans called themselves."

"Ah." Mindy's geek radar went off. This guy was beyond cute, but he was clearly way into the reenactor thing.

"You know, the Puritans believed in blending in too. The Pilgrims and the Puritans came to America about the same time, but the

Pilgrims broke from the Church of England. Puritans stayed inside it, but they changed some of the things about it. They blended in, see?" He smiled openly.

"Ah, okay."

He laughed. "I'm Jasper Gordon," he said. "And you are . . . ?"

"Mindy Gold."

"Ah, I see. Well, Mindy Gold, let me ask you a question. Have you seen a wee lad around here who looks like he doesn't quite belong? Maybe even looks a bit sick like?"

The boy's words went through Mindy's mind. *That guy's a narc, a real dredger. Please don't tell him where I am.*

She hesitated. The boy probably needed help. Hadn't she come here in the first place because that boy seemed like a threat to her sister? But then, she *had* promised the kid—maybe too hastily— that she wouldn't narc on him. He hadn't said or done anything to threaten her, and she had no reason to want to get him in trouble. Besides, who was she to judge him—she didn't know anything about him or what his life was like.

"I saw him," she said, her voice noncommittal. "I can't tell you where he is now."

"Ah, you can't, can't you?" Jasper smiled, his eyes sparkling. "And would you know which way he was headed when last you saw him?"

"I—I really don't know."

Jasper raised an eyebrow, as if he could tell very easily she was lying, but he kept smiling at her and nodding. The thought of his catching her in a lie made Mindy feel flushed and angry, and she tried to think of a sarcastic comeback in case he was about to accuse her of anything.

"Your collar's on backward," he commented.

Mindy blushed. "What are you—some kind of renaissance fair *narc?*" she snapped. She hadn't meant to use the word. It had just slipped out in her anger.

If Jasper minded what she'd said, he didn't show it. "Sure and I take an interest in the past is all. Don't you?" He smiled again.

"Look, it's nice talking to you, but I've really got to go find my sister, okay?"

"Sure, sure. But listen, Mindy Gold. If you see the lad I'm telling you about, steer clear of him, okay? He's bad news. *Believe* me."

"Okay, 'bye!" Mindy said, and turned up the path. She was starting to see how her sister felt about being nagged by authority figures who were really too young to act like authority figures.

Circling around the back of the Governor's House, Mindy found Serena with a cluster of her living-history friends. They were standing in a semicircle, angrily confronting someone out of costume.

It was the boy in the black coat.

Apparently he hadn't left after all. Mindy couldn't quite figure out how he'd gotten around her and arrived at the Governor's House ahead or how he'd gotten into trouble so quickly. But there he was lying on the ground, sweating profusely, and looking pained and embarrassed. Mindy wondered if they had caught him stealing something.

Mindy sped up, gathering her skirt with one hand so she wouldn't trip. "What's going on here?" she demanded, approaching the group. She caught her sister's eye, then looked back at the kid. "I thought you said you were leaving the park." She looked angrily at him.

From about fifty yards away up the gravel path, Jasper shouted. "Step back. Step away from that boy." He began to run toward them.

Serena stepped to the other side of Mindy, and for once her little sister didn't contradict her or give her a hard time. "You'd better just leave," she said. "There's a whole bunch of us and just one of you."

"Hey, what are you reenactor dudes up to now?" Chad's laughter rang out, and Mindy looked over to see him and Veronica walking up the path from the other direction, but they were much closer than Jasper.

"Get back," barked Jasper as he approached them, still at a run, but no one seemed to be listening.

The boy in the black coat looked up at Mindy without straightening up. "I guess I'm about to meet you for the first time in a few minutes."

"Wha—we just met two minutes ago! What is the *matter* with you?"

The kid shrugged. "Details, details." He jammed his left hand into his pocket and pulled out a silver sphere about the size of a golf ball. He raised the sphere over his head and then slammed it onto the ground.

Jasper, just a few feet away now, stretched out his slender arms and lunged toward the kid. Jasper's mouth was open as if to scream, but no sound came out.

With a flash of blinding midnight blue light, Mindy's world went black.

Slow Boats:

4 Reasons to Be Grateful for the Comfort, Convenience, and Safety of Modern Travel

Next time you're miffed about being stuck with a middle seat on that 747, think about the discomforts the colonists suffered crossing the Atlantic in seventeenth-century sailing vessels such as the *Mayflower*. Kinda makes you thankful for that little bag of peanuts, doesn't it?

Reason #1: Passengers were treated like cargo

Seventeenth-century sailing ships were designed to carry cargo, not passengers. On the *Mayflower*, 102 people and their belongings were jammed into a belowdecks chamber a little longer than the base path between home plate and first—and less than one-third that wide. Forget about a window seat: Passengers were offered such amenities as bare wooden floors and windowless plank walls. On some ships, passengers rigged up hammocks and canvas partitions for privacy or sacked out in the longboat on deck for want of room. As for restroom facilities, most ships of the time had a single "head," which was a platform in the bow, or front, of the ship that extended over the water, where passengers and crew did their business. And fresh water was precious, so any washing was done with seawater.

Reason #2: Forget about arriving on time

Seventeenth-century sailing ships had nothing but wind and current to propel them. A typical journey from the port of Plymouth, England, to the Massachusetts coast would take between two and three months, depending on the build and sail capacity of the ship. Travel time depended on the weather. Calm air might bring a ship to a drifting halt, while a stiff breeze from a favorable direction could move up arrival time by days. Encounter a storm, and not only the duration of the journey but also the destination itself would be up for grabs. The *Mayflower* was aiming for the coast of New Jersey but got blown so far off course that it arrived at Cape Cod.

Reason #3: Food service was nonexistent

Ships like the *Mayflower* had a cook onboard, but his job was to feed the crew and the officers, not the passengers. If they wanted a hot meal, passengers were permitted to light a fire in a hibachi-like firebox called a brazier and cook for themselves, but only if the sea was calm. If the sea was rough, the captain forbade fires, and passengers had to settle for cold food.

A typical menu? Salt-cured meat, flour, dried beans, butter, cheese, oil, and beer. After several weeks at sea, water got contaminated, cheese sprouted mold, butter grew rancid, and bugs called weevils infested the flour and the beans. But unless they wanted to go hungry, people had no choice but to eat the spoiled food. As a result, food poisoning was common. Imagine being crammed into a ship's hold full of smelly men, women, and children when the sea wasn't the only thing that was churning.

Reason #4: The turbulence was killer

Passengers on seventeenth-century ships always felt the sea beneath them, as the ships rolled, pitched, and creaked loudly with constant, unpredictable motion. During a storm, waves could rise much higher than the deck, sails had to be lowered, and crew members literally lashed themselves to the masts to avoid being thrown overboard. Even in relatively calm seas, passengers on ships like the *Mayflower* suffered from seasickness for weeks on end.

Chapter Three

Mindy felt as if her stomach had been filled with forty-three grass-hoppers on Red Bull. The insects ricocheted from side to side, all 258 legs evidently fitted with tiny spiked golf shoes. Before she could retch, the spinning jerked to a halt—followed by the sensation of being dropped from a very great height. Leaves and sticks battered her disoriented body before she landed hard on her back.

Jasper Gordon's strangely calm-sounding voice floated toward her. "Mindy Gold? Mindy Gold? Yeh're not dead, are yeh, lass?"

"What happened?" Mindy said, groaning as she opened her eyes to the oppressive midday sun.

Jasper, looking down at her with a concerned expression, shrugged. "Sure and I've no idea in hell."

Mindy scanned the forest around her. Just trees, no dilapidated clapboard house, no surging throng of camera-wielding tourists.

No little sister.

"Serena!" Mindy called.

No answer.

"Serena! Hello?" Mindy reached up reflexively for her scrunchied ponytail. Her fingertips instead brushed a white linen Puritan cap. "Where'd everyone go?"

"Right. They've got to be around here somewhere," Jasper said, appraising the forest around them.

Sweat beaded on Mindy's forehead. It had been forty degrees and midnight when she'd stepped in to defend Serena from that psycho-stalker. Now it had to be seventy, and the sun glared down from directly overhead.

"Wait, what do you mean you *have no idea in hell?*" Mindy asked. "Before that flash of light, you seemed to be the only person who did know what was going on. And you were looking for that kid."

Jasper put his fist in front of his mouth and coughed. "Em. No, sorry, I really don't know. The wee lad just didn't belong there, is all. He looked like he was on drugs, and drugs aren't allowed in Pioneer Village. It's a place for kids and families, you know."

"So what—are you actually a policeman?"

"Ach, now that would be a gas." He laughed. "Sure and did you ever see a policeman in this getup? Nah, I work for the park. I'm not even security or anything—just part of the park administration."

"I see." Mindy was unsure. "We've . . . I've . . . I feel like I've been out a long time," Mindy said.

"It does appear so," Jasper said, patting his clothes as if he'd forgotten something. When his hands reached an oddly shaped lump at his waist, his shoulders relaxed, and he let his hands drop. "To judge by the sun, perhaps as long as twelve hours. And yes, if you're wondering, I've been unconscious the whole time as well."

Mindy didn't like hearing the situation spelled out in such antiseptic terms. Her stomach clenched. "Something's wrong here. If we were unconscious for twelve hours, why didn't someone take us to a hospital or something?" Mindy worked at a veterinary clinic on weekends. She knew no mammal stayed unconscious that long unless something was really wrong with it. Except for being a bit disoriented and woozy, though, she felt okay. "Why wouldn't someone have helped us?"

Jasper shrugged. "Maybe there's nobody left."

"Nobody left? What do you mean by that?"

"I don't know, just that if yer friends didn't take us to the hospital, it must be because they couldn't."

"No. There's got to be a more logical explanation." Mindy went to stick her hands in the pockets of her hoodie only to hit scratchy wool. She tossed her head. No pockets on the stupid dress. "Maybe . . ." she started, "maybe someone dragged us . . . out of the way." She wasn't really sure what she meant by that. "I bet the Governor's House is right on the other side of those woods. We're probably not fifty feet from it. We just can't tell because of the undergrowth." At least that's what she hoped.

"Let's go check it out, then," Jasper said.

The handsome young man's willingness comforted Mindy somewhat. Whatever was going on, they could figure it out together.

Side by side they poked through the woods, walking much farther than Mindy thought they would have to.

Nothing.

"Must be the other side," Mindy said.

They traipsed back across the small clearing and poked through the other side.

Nothing.

They circled the clearing. Not a soul and not a sign of the Governor's House or any of the buildings at Pioneer Village.

"Jasper, where are we?"

A cracking boom echoed in the distance.

"What was that?" Mindy asked, trying to find the source of the sound.

"Em. A gunshot would be my guess," Jasper said.

"There's no hunting allowed in Forest River Park. And it's crawling with tourists, or at least it was. What idiot's got a gun out here?"

"To my ear, that would be a mid-seventeenth-century musket."

Mindy laughed. "That's an ear worthy of Mr. Spock, Jasper." Then it hit her. "Wait—if it's a musket, that means there must be other reenactors still around here. If we walk in the direction of the sound, we should walk right into them."

"Sounds like a right plan," Jasper said.

"Which direction does your Mr. Spock ear tell you the musket shot came from?"

Jasper jerked his head. "Over that way."

Pulling her skirt up past her ankles, Mindy let Jasper lead the way through the undergrowth. "If Serena's anywhere, it'll be where there's a crowd. My sister's such an attention-hog." She sure hoped that was true. She couldn't explain how they'd gotten where they were, or why they'd been out so long without anyone coming to help, but she knew once she found Serena and she was safe, nothing else would matter.

The thick woods closed in all around them, keeping any hope of a breeze from relieving the oppressive heat. How did Serena manage in this getup? The square-toed leather shoes were already creating blisters. The skirt did seem to be warming to her body though, fitting a little better. Guess she had to be thankful for small favors.

Another shot rang out, very close this time. The smell of burning ash and nitrogen tickled Mindy's nose.

"Hold on," she said, rubbing her nose.

Jasper paused, almost bouncing on his heels with excitement. His eyes glittered. "Sure and we're almost there, though! Just a wee bit further, lass."

"Just give me a sec." She breathed deeply, trying to prevent a sneeze.

No good. "Ah-*choo!*"

An angry voice boomed from behind Mindy. "What are you trespassers doing on my land?"

Massachusetts Myths:

6 Common Myths About the New England Colonists

Black and white outfits, Plymouth Rock, and a quest for religious freedom? Well, not quite.

Myth #1: The *Mayflower* passengers landed at Plymouth Rock

The Plymouth Rock landing makes a great origin story, but Plymouth is not the first place where the Pilgrims stepped ashore in the New World (that would be Provincetown, located on the other side of Cape Cod Bay). In Plymouth, they found a site that Wampanoag villagers had cleared for farming and then abandoned. The ready-cleared land and a spring that would be a reliable source of clean water convinced the group leaders that they had found their new home. As for the famous rock? Plymouth Rock only became an object of veneration 121 years after the *Mayflower*, when ninety-five-year-old Thomas Faunce, the town of Plymouth's record keeper, reported that his father, John Faunce, said the Pilgrims first came ashore at the rock. However, records show that John Faunce had not actually been there at the time—he arrived in Plymouth three years after the *Mayflower*, aboard a ship called the *Anne*. Thus the legend of Plymouth Rock is based upon hearsay twice removed.

Myth #2: The Pilgrims called themselves Pilgrims

I say Pilgrim, you say po-*tah*-to. Among the 102 passengers aboard the *Mayflower*, thirty-five were members of the English Separatist Church and were referred to as "Separatists" by their countrymen because they had broken away from the Church of England and were fleeing the religious persecution that resulted. The rest of the passengers were a motley group that included craftsmen, a few experienced military men to provide security, and indentured servants. Today, we lump all of these people together under the term *Pilgrims*, but in fact, the Separatist minority called themselves "saints" and referred to everyone who didn't share their faith as "strangers." It was only in 1820, in a speech to mark the 200th anniversary of the Plymouth Colony's founding, that New Hampshire congressman Daniel Webster, a popular orator, introduced the catchy phrase "Pilgrim Fathers."

Myth #3: Pilgrims dressed in black and white

As any fashionista knows, you can't go wrong with basic black. But the popular image of the Pilgrim in a long black coat with a large, rounded white collar is a serious distortion. No one dressed much like that, at least not for everyday activities. Many residents of the Plymouth Colony wore muted colors, such as soft reddish and brown tones, dark blues, and other hues made from native plant pigments. There was neither an official uniform nor a uniform color. So where does the black and white myth come from? For formal occasions, many residents of Plymouth wore black and white, much as the black tuxedo later became standard formal eveningwear. Simple, non-colored clothing was also favored for church services, especially in the early decades of the colony, because somber clothing was thought to show that the wearer took religion seriously.

Myth #4: Pilgrims and Puritans came to the New World seeking religious freedom

It's true that the Pilgrims fled religious persecution back home in England. It's also true that the Puritans who followed them to Massachusetts within a few years fled religious discrimination by English church and state officials. But the last thing either of these groups wanted was religious *freedom* the way we understand it today. Both groups believed that society should be ruled by a strict, Bible-based interpretation of God's law. The Pilgrim and Puritan sects were enough alike that their members in Massachusetts blended without much trouble. But anyone unwilling to worship and live according to Pilgrim/Puritan values, or anyone who publicly disagreed with their ideas, was not welcome.

Myth #5: The Puritans abstained from alcohol

Actually, the Puritans were far from, er, puritan when it came to drinking. Everybody, including children, drank beer, even for breakfast. They thought of it more as a source of nutrition than as a buzz-inducing refreshment. The beer-as-food tradition started in the old country, where drinking water was often a dangerous source of many illnesses, including deadly typhoid fever. Beer and ale, on the other hand, were known to be safer. Colonial housewives brewed their own, usually a variety called *small beer,* which was relatively low in alcohol content. Because brewing tended to take over the kitchen hearth, many colonists built a small addition to their houses, usually on the cooler north side of the structures, strictly for making beer. Wine—homemade from native berries or imported from Europe—was also popular.

Myth #6: New England colonists were against slavery

We think of the South as the hotbed of American slavery and New England as the center of the anti-slavery movement before the Civil War. But Massachusetts was a slaveholding colony as early as 1624, when an Englishman named Samuel Maverick arrived in Plymouth with two African slaves. Although there were colonists who found slaveholding repugnant, most residents of Plymouth Colony and Massachusetts Bay Colony had no qualms about the buying and selling of human beings. New England traders actually dominated the slave trade during the late 1600s and early 1700s: By the 1670s, Boston ships were taking on cargoes of slaves in Madagascar and selling them in Virginia. Massachusetts-based ships also brought human cargo from Africa to the West Indies, where the captains traded slaves for sugar, rum, and other goods that they could sell at a profit. Many colonists kept slaves themselves, but New England slavery never matched the scale of slavery in the Southern colonies. The hilly, rocky landscape of New England was not suited for large plantation-scale agriculture, so small family farms dominated. Farmers who could afford to would have at most a slave or two to help with the fieldwork and another to help in the house. Most Massachusetts slaves worked as house servants in the cities. In the 1780s, after the Revolutionary War, the Massachusetts Supreme Court ruled that the commonwealth's new constitution guaranteed freedom without regard to race, effectively outlawing slavery.

Chapter Four

Mindy looked down the long barrel of an antique musket. Peering at her over the top of the gun was a very angry-looking middle-aged man dressed in quite authentic-looking colonial garb. The man's brown doublet had loops instead of buttons, and his breeches were made of leather. His face was extremely wrinkled, and he looked like he'd spent far too much time out in the sun playing colonial farmer. Mindy had seen his type before. She would have thought this man was old enough to know better than to accost an outsider with his musket, but he seemed, unaccountably, to be genuinely angry at her.

Mindy glanced to the figure at his side. A tall, well-muscled young man with shoulder-length black hair and smoldering emerald eyes, the second reenactor was dressed more impressively in a snugly tailored forest green suit, his shirt collar wrapped around his throat like a scarf and tucked into his doublet. He held a black book under his arm that gave him a ministerial cast, but with his chiseled features and flowing hair, he looked like he belonged on the cover of some tawdry romance novel with a buxom woman clutching his ripped midsection. The younger man looked back and forth awkwardly between his companion and Mindy, seemingly embarrassed by the older man's behavior.

But Mindy had had enough—this jackass was actually pointing a live firearm at her. Before the younger man could say anything, she looked the older man in the face defiantly and barked, "You're pointing a loaded gun at me?! What are you—*insane?*" She could barely contain the fury in her voice. "I don't think it's really appropriate for you to point that at me, even if it is four hundred years old."

The handsome young man with the book spoke up. "'Tis a woman, brother Gargery." His tone was smooth and soothing yet commanding—the kind of voice one might use to address a skittish horse. "Let us use the reason God gave us and discuss this matter amicably."

The old farmer lowered his weapon and spat on the ground. "Pah! God never *gave* me what I didn't work long and hard for, and I'll not stand still while others come and take the land away from me. Nigh two year I worked these stony fields, pulling up the rocks with my bare hands so the plow would travel, and only on the third did it yield a puny harvest—little enough for m'wife and bairns. And then old man Putnam dies and leaves *my* fields—Gargery Walford's fields—to *his* son Thomas—a canker of a man who never pulled rock nor stone out of any place. I'll see him in the grave before he takes my farm." He spat again and glanced at Mindy and Jasper. "And now these two come snooping about my lands. Tell me this, missy: When did *you* pull rocks out of anything?"

The young man interjected. "Come, come, brother Gargery," he said with a hearty laugh. "You've no reason to think they've done anything wrong. It's not as if you caught them sneaking the rocks back into your fields."

Mindy thought it was time to speak up again. "Listen, do you mind if we drop this reenactment act for just a minute to discuss an urgent matter?"

The old man's eyes popped out in rage. "I'll not be back-talked to on m'own farm—the farm that I took the rocks out of *stone by stone*—by a sassy young thing like yourself. I'll see you flogged in the town square!"

Mindy rolled her eyes. What was with this guy and his rocks? "Look, just don't talk to me, okay? I'll get off *your land* right now. You couldn't pay me to watch your dumb reenactment."

Mindy turned abruptly and began walking away with swift determination. She just had to get her bearings—surely if she got to the top of that hill she would see the town or a street that she recognized and see where she was.

Behind her, she heard Jasper's apologetic voice speaking in low tones. "I must beg ye be so kind as not to notice me sister's disordered speech. She suffers severely from an affliction of the mind and temperament. When we travel to a new place she becomes confused and hostile. 'Tis been her way since she was a child."

Mindy's blood boiled. What the hell was Jasper doing playing these colonial games? Serena was missing, and Mindy badly needed to find a phone and call her mother and figure out just what the hell was going on. She was starting to get the feeling that this guy was a nut, and she wasn't going to wait around for him.

In the distance she heard old farmer Gargery coughing and wheezing. "Don't think you can get away that easy, missy. I've cleared the rocks out of every inch of this hillside and know it like me own hand." Yet he did indeed seem to fall behind as Mindy reached the crest of the hill, his pants and wheezes growing fainter.

Mindy looked around her in astonishment. For what seemed to be miles around, she saw unbroken fields and forests, without so much as a road or street lamp, telephone or electrical wire. No airplanes flew in the brilliant blue sky above her.

Before she had time to process the fact that she was farther from home than she'd thought, she felt a tugging at her sleeve and looked down into the pleading eyes of a young girl in colonial garb. The girl had dirty blond hair and wore a coarse, worn, woolen garment. She looked up at Mindy with her big blue eyes, pointing a finger toward some bushes as she dragged Mindy along with her.

Mindy followed, protesting weakly. "Wait, I'm not really part of this reenactment. I don't work here. I don't *belong* here."

She stopped short as she saw where the child was taking her. Lying on its side in the bushes, panting weakly, was an enormous black wolfhound, bleeding from a gunshot wound in its side. The dog, a female, mutely turned her eyes up at Mindy.

Mindy dropped to her knees beside the dog, her trained hands feeling along the dog's ribcage to gauge the extent of the damage. The wound was on the dog's left ventral side, near the kidney, and was bleeding rapidly. *I need to apply pressure to this with a bandage,* she thought. But the fabric of her dress did not look easy to tear.

Panting and wheezing, farmer Gargery stumbled into view, his young companion and Jasper right behind him. "Becca!" He said to the girl. "I thought I left you by the old path to the farmhouse, collecting the smaller stones for me to use in me rock garden."

"This dog has been shot," Mindy said, thinking, *Again, the damn rocks.* It seemed clear enough who had shot it, but Mindy wasn't going to gain anything by confronting the crazed farmer. "She needs medical attention. I need a phone. Can someone please give me a phone?"

The farmer looked at her stupidly. She glanced up at his tall companion, who also looked confused, but who looked strong enough to lift and carry the dog. "Will you help me, please?" Mindy looked into his eyes. The young man knelt down beside her by the dog. "Help me get her into a house. We might be able to save her."

The young man's voice was gentle. "Farmer Gargery's house is very near. We can take it there. I am Minister Jonathan Hartthorne— Gargery Walford's brother-in-law. Forgive our harsh greeting. You will find a better welcome here than you have thus far, I promise you." He cradled the big dog in his strong arms and led Mindy back down the hill.

"I know that dog," muttered farmer Gargery. "'Tis Thomas Putnam's dog! The big black devil. Many a time have it come prowling about me farm, looking to carry off me wee 'uns." The farmer trailed behind Mindy and the minister, muttering to Jasper, who encouraged him with appreciative comments and questions.

Minister Hartthorne led them back to a remarkably authentic-looking colonial New England farmhouse. The walls of the dwelling were white clapboard, and the windows were small with diamond-shaped panes. A barn and outhouse stood off to one side, and a well-maintained vegetable garden peaked out from behind the building.

The minister led the way into an austere main room with wide floorboards and simple wooden furniture. An imposing fireplace spanned the center wall of the house, its heat radiating throughout the room. What little light filtered through the small windows gave the rough-hewn oak ceiling beams and the rest of the room a pale gray-green tinge.

In front of the fire, the minister set down the suffering dog, and Mindy quickly knelt down to attend to it. She dispatched the minister to the kitchen for towels and hot water, but even a cursory examination revealed to Mindy's trained eye that the dog didn't have long to live. As it whimpered in pain, Mindy's competent hands shifted the animal into a more comfortable position and soothed it with smooth strokes to its broad forehead. Under her hands, the dog relaxed, and soon after, it died.

Despite having seen animals suffer and die before, Mindy had never gotten used to it. She felt her eyes welling with tears.

Farmer Gargery softened at the sight of Mindy tending to the poor animal. "Ach, I can't deny the girl has a kind heart, though indeed she's loony as a jaybird."

Mindy ignored the idiot farmer and listened to the calm, soothing voice of the minister talking to Jasper near the doorway to the kitchen. She realized they were talking about her.

"Your sister said the word *reenactment,* as if she thought we were all engaged in doing something . . . that had already happened." The minister was speaking in a low voice, unaware that Mindy was listening. "She talks as if she thinks we're all *actors.* 'Tis a strange malady she suffers from—though she does seem to know what she's about with the animal."

"Em. Yes, animals have always been a consolation to her spirit. But you must excuse us—we can't be staying long—"

"Jasper." Mindy's voice was sharp. She had had enough of this nonsense. It was time to find her sister—or at least a responsible, sane adult. Charming accent or not, she had known Jasper for exactly fifteen minutes, not counting the twelve hours they apparently lay unconscious together, and she didn't think that justified his making up stories about her life and medical history to some reenactors. "Jasper, do you in fact have any idea where we are or how we got here?"

Jasper reddened and, after a pause, spoke: "Er, do you mean

whose farm is this in particular? Now I think we've pretty well established that farmer Gargery—"

"No, jackass. I mean what happened to Salem City? Why are we
stuck out here in the middle of nowhere in reenactment-land?"

Now all three men looked embarrassed, shuffling their feet
uneasily and not meeting her eyes. "Eh, no, Mindy," Jasper said.
"Sure and I really don't. But look, my new friends," he said, turning to the two men, "would it be acceptable if we had just a little
refreshment—catch our breath a bit before heading on? This has all
been very exciting. Farmer Gargery, is that a jug of hard cider I see
over there? And a loaf of bread? Might I have the honor of pouring a
libation in your honor?"

Mindy eyed Jasper narrowly as Gargery murmured his gruff
assent and passed the bread to her. Jasper poured cider into rough
pewter cups, humming nonchalantly to himself. *What the hell is up
with this guy—or with any of these people?* Mindy thought, tearing
into the bread.

Then something caught her eye. Something was just not quite
right about the way Jasper was holding one of the cups. What was he
doing? Then there it was—she distinctly saw a clear fluid slip from
his hand into the cup along with the cider.

Jasper had put something in her drink.

Colonial Cuisine:

6 Common Foods in Seventeenth-Century New England

Ah, food. The topic never fails to fascinate. Everyone needs it, and just about everyone has strong opinions on it. Long before the days of Taco Bell and twenty-four-hour pizza delivery, putting food on the table with regularity was no simple matter: If you wanted to eat it, you had to either grow or kill it.

Food #1: Corn

Serving suggestions: *roasted corn, corn mush, cornmeal, popcorn, cornbread*

Corn for breakfast, lunch, and dinner, anyone? In colonial New England, native corn—or "Indian corn," as it was initially called—quickly became a diet staple. When the Pilgrims landed in New England, one of the first things they stumbled upon, according to written accounts, was a mound of earth left by local Native Americans that was a storage place for corn. The next spring, the English-speaking Squanto showed the Pilgrims how to grow their own corn and fertilize it by putting a whole fish in the ground with each seed. The colonists discovered the native grain to be an incredibly versatile, nutritious—not to mention delicious—food source.

Food #2: Barley and wheat

Serving suggestions: *wheat bread, pancakes, barley porridge, beer*

Although the colonists quickly developed a taste for corn, they still longed for the familiar breads and cakes they had enjoyed back in England. Unfortunately, the wheat and barley seeds they brought with them grew poorly in the rocky Massachusetts soil. This was especially bad news for colonial beer drinkers because barley is a main ingredient in beer. Partly because the colonists yearned so much for a cold one, barley became one of the first commodities they imported from England, along with hops, also an ingredient used to make beer. As years passed, colonists developed wheat varieties that produced better crops, but it was several decades before they could get the more delicate barley to thrive.

Food #3: Squash and beans

Serving suggestions: *roasted squash, pumpkin pie, pumpkin seeds, baked beans*

What would Thanksgiving be without good old pumpkin pie? It's hard to believe, but before they came to New England, colonists had never enjoyed the sweet, sweet taste of pumpkin pie (they also hadn't celebrated a Thanksgiving yet, but that's another story). Native Americans taught the colonists how to grow and prepare a variety of native beans and squash varieties, plants that flourished in the Massachusetts soil. Soon, pumpkin pie became as American as . . .

Food #4: Eels and other slimy things from the sea

Serving suggestions: *fish stew, clam chowder, roast eel, eel stew*

Fish always had been a part of the English diet, but in New England the colonists encountered an abundance of fishy foods the likes of which they had never seen before. During the first year at Plymouth, colonists indulged in everything from Atlantic salmon to cod to clams. They liked eels best of all, probably because Squanto had shown them an easy way to catch these long, snakelike fish by using a baited trap-basket woven from twigs. Although they've fallen out of favor as a food source, eels at the time were considered good eats.

Food #5: Deer, ducks, turkey, and other wild game

Serving suggestions: *roast turkey, roast duck, roast goose, roast rabbit*

The colonists quickly found hunting to be an efficient way to put dinner on the table, and New England presented them with better hunting than they had ever known before. Wild game, such as deer, duck, turkey, and rabbit, was far more plentiful in the New World than in England, where centuries of agriculture had displaced many square miles of woods and fields. The Pilgrims carried stores of firearms with them on the *Mayflower*, and records show that the only animals aboard the ship were two hunting dogs: an English mastiff and an English spaniel.

Food #6: Salt

Serving suggestions: *salt pork, salt goat, salt beef, salt fish, salt venison*

Sure, it tastes delicious on French fries, but in the seventeenth century, salt was most useful as a food preservative. Before the invention of refrigerators, meats and fish could be kept for long periods only if they were carefully dried and treated with salt. After butchering a goat or pig, colonists would cut the meat into strips and plunge them into a bin of salt, where they sat for up to a month. Next, the strips would be hung in a special smokehouse, where the heat finished the drying process and chemicals in the smoke acted as preservatives. The finished product could be kept for months—even a year or two—without going bad.

Chapter Five

Mindy froze in mid-bite, a lump of bread still in her mouth. She still had no idea what was going on, but now she knew for certain that Jasper was not to be trusted.

"No thanks," she said in a measured tone, "I don't drink alcohol." She swallowed hard.

"Now she won't take my cider, she says," Gargery grumbled.

Jasper turned around, carefully steadying the new concoction in his pretty little hands, and found Mindy's wide eyes staring him in the face. The look of fear and contempt they held seemed to startle Jasper. He dropped the pewter mug to the floor, its contents quickly disappearing through the cracks in the wood. Flustered, Jasper looked first to Mindy, then darted his eyes between the pitying minister and the fuming farmer, "Eh, I'm truly sorry. I, em, don't know—"

"Deliver me, are ye all batty?" Gargery thundered. "There's work to be done in this house, and I don't have time to bander about with touched-off maidens and bumbling oafs!"

"Patience, brother Gargery—they're obviously both overwrought," the minister soothed. "Miss Mindy, are you well?"

Mindy's eyes hadn't left Jasper and hadn't lost their look of rising panic, as she slowly backed toward the rear door. The minister's calm voice relaxed her for a moment. But on turning to see his dusted and disheveled green cloak and the menacing, wrinkled flesh of the red-faced farmer behind him, her resolve quickened. Acting or not, these people were deranged and maybe even dangerous. She felt like she was in a colonial version of *Alice in Wonderland,* and she was going to get out, now.

Mindy turned and bolted out the door. She could hear Jasper's feeble protests, but nothing was going to keep her in this nuthouse another second. She stumbled down the uneven steps and slid as her foot hit mud, landing in a heap in the yard. The squawking of geese filled her ears. Suddenly, a barking dog was very near her face. She stood up and took the scene in at a glance.

Two young girls, the first maybe two or three years old and the other a couple of years older, both in drab, stiff-looking cotton dresses, were bent over to her right pulling weeds from what looked like a vegetable garden. A woman who couldn't have been more than twenty-five, although the stern features of her face seemed to add innumerable years to her, was squatting on a log in front of Mindy. An errant lock of blond hair had escaped her close-fitting white linen cap and was hanging in front of her eyes. Bits of down covered her faded violet skirt. Tucked under her arm was a struggling bundle of white feathers.

"Don't just stand there, girl," the woman said with a huff. "Don't be useless . . . round me up another goose." With that, the woman struck a hand down onto the bird she was holding and pulled up, with a violent, deliberate gesture, a fistful of feathers.

Cringing, Mindy looked away. "Aren't you going to kill it first?"

"Don't be foolish. The feathers will grow back before winter, and we can do it all over again in the spring."

The chunk of rye bread sloshed uncomfortably in Mindy's stomach, threatening to crawl up her throat. The woman plucked another handful of feathers from the quivering goose and deposited it into a sack at her feet. Down, like oversized snowflakes, hung in the air all around her, slowly drifting to the ground. With each pluck, the goose jerked. The woman gestured at the stump opposite Mindy. "Well, if you're going to help, grab a goose and get to it."

Mindy stammered, "I think I'm going to be sick." The sight of such vivid animal cruelty caused a wave of nausea to roll upward as her stomach gurgled downward. Her shoulders slumped, and she tried to breathe deeply, but she couldn't block out the sound of the struggling goose and the barking dog. Behind her, she heard footsteps. In a daze, she looked around to see Jasper slowly moving down the steps and the minister filling the doorway to the house.

The woman muttered shortly, "Never mind, then," and out the corner of her eye, Mindy saw the woman grab another goose and shove a wicker cone over the animal's head.

"Mindy, girl, please just calm down. Sure and there's a simple explanation for all of this," Jasper said. Rather than malice, Mindy thought she could detect genuine concern in his voice. His movements were slow and hesitant, and his eyes held a look of plaintive concern.

But the whole scene was more than Mindy could swallow. Where was she? Where were all the regular people? What was with these fanatical reenactors? Her sister was missing, she was stranded God knows where, she was wearing extremely uncomfortable clothes, and no one had a cell phone or even a landline. *Sheesh, a pay phone would be a godsend at this point!* she thought. Mindy put her hand to her head and grabbed at her hair. She didn't even have a scrunchy! For some reason, although trivial compared to everything else that had happened in the past half hour, this last realization sent her over the edge. Fear flashed to fury. She was going to get out of here, and she was going to report each and every one of these people, even the hunky minister, to the police and the ASPCA.

A plump, milky-white goose appeared at Mindy's feet, its long neck bobbing interestedly at the scrap of bread she still held in her hand. Suddenly a dozen birds surrounded her. Mindy dropped the bread and the geese surged, forming an undulating gray and white circle around her.

Their movements hypnotized her, and she couldn't turn her head. The birds' heads and necks moved like snakes emerging from white, feathered, egglike bodies. As she watched, frozen amid the frenzy, the long necks of the geese detached from their bodies and slithered toward her toes.

Mindy screamed.

A goose-headed snake slithered around her foot and slid beneath her heavy wool skirt. Mindy pulled at the multiple layers of petticoats, shaking them and kicking her legs. Jasper, Minister Hartthorne, and the woman were rooted to their spots. Wasn't anyone going to help?

Mindy picked up one of the fist-sized rocks lining the garden by her feet and threw it into the mass of wings and bills.

"Argh! Where'd that rock come from? Not agaaaaiiin!" Gargery's wailing voice rushed in from somewhere in the chaos and then seemed to zoom away.

Another white serpentine head slithered over Mindy's foot and curled around her ankle. Its bill slowly opened to reveal a pair of fangs, dripping with heavy green saliva. Its black eyes grew into shimmering, wavering pools of darkness. The distorted wails of the geese reverberated all around her. Mindy's own screams seemed to detach from her body and blend in with the hollow din. As she watched the sharp fangs sink into her skin, she felt nothing. Nothing at all. She was now drifting into the inky blackness of the goose-snake's eye. The sound that was now surrounding her became muffled and dull. Everything went black.

Massachusetts Maladies:

3 Deadly Diseases in Seventeenth-Century New England

Before the wonders of modern medicine, everyday symptoms like chills, fevers, and weight loss often meant that death was just around the corner.

Disease #1: Smallpox

Prognosis: *slow, painful death by internal bleeding; uncontrolled high fever; pneumonia; secondary bacterial infection*

In the 1600s, smallpox killed many thousands worldwide, including residents of the towns and villages of colonial Massachusetts. Symptoms progressed from chills and fever to hard, red lumps that became painful blisters. If the victim survived, the blisters left permanent pitted scars. Because smallpox had afflicted Europeans for centuries, many English had some degree of resistance. The death rate among the English colonists who caught the disease was rarely higher than 30 percent. For the Native Americans, however, it was an entirely different story: It is thought that 90 percent of those who contracted it died, and whole tribes were wiped out. William Bradford, governor of the Plymouth Colony, wrote that Native Americans with smallpox "die like rotten sheep." Today, smallpox has been eradicated through modern medicine, and public health officials see no need even to vaccinate Americans against the once-feared disease.

Disease #2: Scurvy

Prognosis: *slow, painful death by internal bleeding*

When your mom told you to eat your fruits and vegetables, she wasn't kidding around. Go too long without the green stuff, and you're likely to come down with a case of scurvy. This is precisely what happened to about half the Pilgrims during their first winter in Massachusetts, when they survived on a vegetable-free diet of freshly hunted game and *Mayflower* leftovers, including salt-cured meats and wheat flour. Many suffered bleeding gums, tooth loss, painful joints, and festering sores that would not heal—all symptoms of scurvy. In all, more than fifty out of about 125 passengers and crew died during that first winter, some of scurvy and some of a combination of scurvy and other diseases. The simplest preventive measure? Eat oranges and leafy vegetables. Scurvy is now known to be caused by a lack of vitamin

C, which is prevalent in citrus fruits. Even in the 1600s, Native Americans made a tea of certain evergreen leaves in the winter, and colonists learned from Dutch sailors about using lime juice to get through winters scurvy-free.

Disease #3: Tuberculosis

Prognosis: *slow, painful death by coughing*

The colonists lived in fear of sudden weight loss, as it was often an early sign of what they called consumption, the lung infection that we know today as tuberculosis. Along with sudden and drastic weight loss, victims of tuberculosis developed a persistent cough. Because it often mimics other diseases, such as pneumonia, and could go undiagnosed, there's no way to know just how prevalent tuberculosis was among the residents of seventeenth-century New England. Worldwide, it was a leading cause of death. Victims could often carry the bacteria for years and even decades without symptoms. When they began to cough blood, however, it usually meant that death was a year or two away. Victims eventually lost the ability to breathe as their lungs filled up with blood.

Chapter Six

Mindy woke up in her bed, wrapped up in her comfortable cotton jersey sheets. The rose-colored down comforter that her mother had given her two winters ago felt soft and warm, cradling her body like a cloud. The morning sunlight was peeking through her bedroom window, creating a halo around the leaves of the maple tree outside. The rays seemed to tickle her nose, cheeks, and eyelids. She let out a heavy sigh and smiled.

Rolling over, she saw her sister sitting on the white wicker chair on the other side of the room. She was dressed in a petticoat and an olive-colored waistcoat. She was putting on a pair of square leather shoes.

"Where are you going?" Mindy's voice was playful, soft, and lazy, slipping effortlessly out of her lips.

"Sure and it's time, Mindy. We have to get going. It's time." Serena's lips seemed to move ahead of the sound they made. "It's time, Mindy."

"Time? But what time is it?" Mindy was trying to shake the fog from her mind.

"It's time, Mindy. We have to go."

Mindy was startled, but she couldn't move. Serena rose from her chair. She spoke, but her voice sounded different. It was lilting and musical—a man's voice. There was something strangely familiar about it. Mindy couldn't place it, but it struck fear into her. Serena's hand reached out for her and grabbed her forearm. "Mindy, me lass. C'mere and wake up, girl. It's time we were going." Mindy shut her eyes tight.

A soft, small hand was holding tight to her wrist. "Sure and it's time, Mindy girl. We've got to be *going*." The voice was quick and hushed but very clear. It was Jasper, and he was kneeling next to her head.

Mindy was lying on a strange bed. It was stiff, as if only an inch of loose padding separated her from the box spring. The room around her was plain—the walls were just bare wood. There was only one window. Off to the right of the bed was a doorway. Standing in front of the doorway was the imposing body of farmer Gargery, arms folded across his barreled chest and a stone look on his face.

"Let go of me!" Mindy shouted, attempting to twist out of Jasper's tight grasp.

"Mindy, please trust me, girl. We need to *go*."

Trust Jasper? The little man she'd just caught trying to slip her poison only moments before a flock of rabid geese began to eat her?

"Call the police! Someone, call for help!" Mindy sat up, shaking.

"I would think a doctor would be more appropriate." The voice was that of Minister Hartthorne, who was kneeling at her other side.

"A doctor, yes, perfect. That would be fantastic!" Mindy was so relieved that finally someone was making sense.

"T'aint need for a doctor here, Brother Jonathan," Gargery said. "We need to fetch the constable."

Good God, don't these people let up, Mindy thought. She couldn't believe this guy was still going at it. She felt her eyes burn as a desperate frustration began to rush to her head and face.

"Now, Brother Gargery," Hartthorne urged, "common charity demands that we address any ailments this poor dear is suffering. You saw her actions. She's in need of our assistance."

"But I saw her tearing rocks out of the earth and running about like a fool!"

Hartthorne disregarded Gargery's comment and turned to Jasper. "Friend Jasper, did this latest episode come on similar to those in the past?"

"Well," Jasper fumbled, "Sure and they're all a wee bit different, I should think. But what the dear girl always seems to find most soothing to her spirits is a solitary walk. Let me just go about with her a bit, and I'm sure she'll be fine."

"Fine my foot! I see what you're doing." Gargery stepped forward. "Don't think I don't see what you two are about. First Parris's daughter, then the Putnam girl. Do ye think I'm stupid? I tell ye, Brother Hartthorne, we need the constable here. He'll know how to make this right."

"Are you all crazy?" Mindy screamed. "This is a nightmare. If you're not going to get me a doctor, then I'm getting the hell out of here!"

"Em. Right, Mindy, let's get you out of here," Jasper said, starting to rise.

"Get away from me, you lunatic." Mindy shoved his arm away with withering scorn. "I'm not going anywhere with you, you little roofie-slipping Irish bastard. That *was* Rohypnol you tried to give me, wasn't it?" she hissed. "I guess you're too *little* to kidnap a girl without pharmaceutical assistance."

"Rose hips. That's good, Miss Mindy. That may help to soothe you," the minister jumped in. "If we don't have some, I'm sure the apothecary does. But first, we need to determine your symptoms. There's surely a reasonable explanation for what has happened to you."

Mindy couldn't think. Her mind was racing. She felt as if someone was trying to pull her intestines out through her throat. Was she the one who was crazy? What happened in the yard wasn't normal. It wasn't real. Nothing like that had ever happened to her before. And these people—why wouldn't they just help her? Hot tears started to come to her eyes.

"Oh, I think I can give you a reasonable explanation," Gargery said in a low voice.

"Don't say it, brother." Hartthorne rose to his feet. "There's enough of that going on right now. We must keep our heads. God works in mysterious ways, but His path is always marked by reason."

"A pox on your reason, Jonathan," Gargery growled. "God also has enemies. And when those enemies reveal themselves, it's our duty to take notice. See here now, we're going to fetch the constable. This girl is bewitched!"

Mindy closed her eyes. Tears began to stream out.

Bad Medicine:

5 Scary Seventeenth-Century Treatments for Common Ailments

Human urine, pig dung, and bug parts? So much for "take two aspirin and call me in the morning."

Treatment #1: Bleeding

Used to treat: *scarlet fever, flu, sore throat, infections, various illnesses*

Scared of needles? Be thankful you didn't live in seventeenth-century New England, where a doctor's lancet (small knife) was his favorite tool. Doctors would use their lancets to slice open a patient's vein, allowing a pint or even more of the patient's blood to flow into a basin. This centuries-old treatment was considered good medicine for a variety of ailments, including a run-of-the-mill fever, infections, and general listlessness. In a different, similarly bloody procedure, live leeches were placed on a patient's skin next to a wound to help speed up the healing. Although we now know that bloodletting with a lancet did absolutely no good (and probably caused a good deal of harm in most cases), modern researchers have discovered that treating patients with leeches actually helps improve blood circulation to a wound.

Treatment #2: Poison

Used to treat: *scarlet fever, flu, sore throat, infections, various other illnesses*

Seventeenth-century doctors believed it was effective to empty out a sick person's digestive system—from both ends. The treatment? Poison. Many of the emetic and purgative medicines doctors used to induce vomiting or diarrhea contained substances that we'd classify as poisons today. The most widely used medicine of the time, calomel, was actually mercury chloride—a toxic compound used today to kill fungi. Long-term exposure to its component element, mercury, damages the human nervous system and can cause mental illness. Another medicine, tartar emetic, contained the heavy metal antimony, which also poses a dire health risk.

Treatment #3: Bug powder

Used to treat: *swollen glands, jaundice, nosebleeds*

Many seventeenth-century home remedies called for patients to eat, drink, or sniff bug parts. One such "cure" involved soaking a handful of pill bugs in white port wine for several days. After the bugs were strained out, the resulting solution was used in the treatment of swollen glands and for jaundice, a common liver disorder. For lung infections, people often turned to concoctions such as powdered millipedes in donkey's milk or pulverized crayfish in horse's milk. Nosebleeds were treated with spiders, which were tied up in a rag and sniffed.

Treatment #4: Hair of a virgin

Used to treat: *labor pains, difficult childbirths*

In seventeenth-century New England, as many as two out of every 100 childbirths ended in the mother's death. If those odds don't sound terrible, consider that the average married woman could expect to have eight children. For difficult labors, a midwife might try to ease pain and speed up the delivery by taking the following steps:

1. Find a virgin at least half the age of the woman in labor and cut a lock of her hair.
2. Take twelve ant eggs, dry them, and grind them into a powder.
3. Mix ant egg powder with virgin hair in one-fourth of a pint of milk from a red cow (if a red cow isn't available, ale wort may be used as a substitute).
4. Get the woman in childbirth to drink the concoction.

Treatment #5: Excrement

Used to treat: *nosebleeds, jaundice, palsy, blisters*

Warning: If you're squeamish, stop reading now. Still here? Okay, don't say we didn't warn you. Nosebleeds were sometimes treated with fresh pig dung rolled into two cone-shaped plugs and shoved up the nostrils. Human waste also featured in home remedies. One treatment for jaundice called for the patient to drink his or her own urine every morning and evening. One prominent seventeenth-century Salem physician, Dr. Zerobabel Endecott, put his stamp of approval on the treatment when he wrote that the "volatile fat of urine" was effective in combating jaundice. Suffering from palsy (involuntary shaking)? If you were living in seventeenth-century New England, your doctor might have advised you to take a bath in hot urine and absinthe, a green-tinted alcoholic drink that is illegal in the United States today because of its potency.

Chapter Seven

Jasper was holding his head in his hands, muttering in exaspera-tion. "Shite and tobacco plants. I can't believe I bolloxed things up this badly."

"Don't trouble yourself, friend Jasper. All will be right." Hartthorne held out his hands in protest as he turned to Gargery. "We do not need the constable, brother. You know what that will bring. Let us first approach this with sense. A doctor can examine her, then we shall see what is what."

"Sense? Was it sense that let that Indian woman, Tituba, bewitch those children? Ye may see fit to prattle about with a bunch of beakers and tools, scribbling pictures of plants and calling it *reason,* but I tell you the constable has ways of getting to the bottom of this. Or maybe," Gargery said with a scornful glance at Hartthorne's leafy, disheveled hair, "ye'll want to go finding your answers among some leaves and shrubs!"

Hartthorne brought himself up. "There's no need for ugliness, brother. I'm only trying to use the tools God gave me. This girl is sick, I tell you."

"There's other girls been sick in this town. I tell you, dark omens are afoot. I'll not let spirits enter my own house unchallenged!"

Mindy felt her fingers and toes begin to tingle, almost as if someone were pinching her. She shivered uncontrollably.

"What is it?" Minister Hartthorne asked, noticing her shaking. "Mindy, look at me. Are you well?"

Mindy looked at him. His emerald eyes looked calm and inviting. They seemed to expand ever so slightly. Mindy opened her mouth, but she couldn't respond. She felt like a stone sinking to the bottom of the ocean.

Far away, she heard Jasper's voice: "Jasper, me boy, ye've made a right bags of this, ye have." Then everything went black.

As her eyes slowly opened, the hazy surroundings took on form. For the second time, Mindy awoke to find herself in the same strange bed, in the same strange room, surrounded by the same strange people. How long had she been asleep? Was it hours? Days? And how was she going to get out of here?

"She had another fit right there in that bed. I tell you, Constable Roberts, she's been made the victim of witchcraft. Something has to be done!"

"In due time, Neighbor Gargery, in due time," a high-pitched, nasal voice said. "I assure you that this matter is most serious, and we will make haste to ensure your safety by what means may be necessary."

Mindy's eyes adjusted to take in farmer Gargery, arms gesturing, speaking to another man. This new man was short and plump. He wore a black shirt and black trousers, similar to Gargery's, only on this man they were stretched to bursting across his massive belly and legs. His face was red and shiny, like an ugly baby. An overly serious expression along with a stubby nose and tiny black eyes made him look like a cartoon. Under any other circumstances Mindy might have been tempted to giggle.

"Constable Roberts, with humble respect, I would suggest that what this girl really needs is a doctor. Please, let us use reason," Hartthorne said.

"Duly noted, minister. Doctor Griggs has been sent for and should be arriving shortly."

Relief washed over Mindy at the mention of a doctor. Finally, someone who would help her. But her relief diminished when she saw the disappointed look on Hartthorne's face. He turned to her with what she could clearly tell was pity, and he shook his head. Evidently this Griggs character wouldn't be much of an improvement.

"Gentlemen, I can assure you I'll clear this nonsense up if you'll leave me alone with my sister for just a minute." The sound of Jasper's musical voice shook the cobwebs from Mindy's head.

"NO!" she shouted. "Do not leave me with him. He's not my brother! Do we *look* like we belong together? I don't know who he is, but he just tried to poison me. Or maybe he did poison me? I don't know, but he's insane—do *not* leave me with him."

"Right. Ah, Mindy, no. You don't know what you're saying," Jasper pleaded in a whisper.

"Don't talk to me. Someone, help me, please!"

"What is the meaning of this?" Constable Roberts exclaimed with impatience. "Just what's going on here?"

"This is Jasper Gordon, constable," Hartthorne informed, "the brother of the afflicted girl—or so I thought."

Mindy began to shout. "How many times do I have to say it? I am not afflicted with anything! And he is not my brother! He's a madman, and he needs to be locked up with the rest of you."

"Quiet please, miss," the constable said with annoyance.

"Aye, afflicted she is." Gargery leaned in toward the constable. "She's bewitched. You should have seen her among my rocks."

"Enough!" Mindy stood up in the bed. "No more acting! No more games! No more colonial Salem witchcraft mumbo-jumbo nonsense! I want my sister, and I want to go home!"

"Oh my, her case is rather advanced." The voice came from a man standing in the doorway. He was short and thin, with sunken cheekbones and a nervousness about him that made Mindy instantly uncomfortable. Remembering Hartthorne's look, she feared who he might be.

"Doctor Griggs, excellent," the constable said, ushering him in. "See now, these men charge that she's been having episodes. Seeing strange visions, screeching like a she-wolf, and tossing her body about."

"And she's let loose on my geese and ripped asunder my rock garden!" Gargery added.

"But her condition has somewhat subsided," Hartthorne offered. "Her visions have passed. I feel she may have eaten something disagreeable, and that is all."

"Nothing looks passed to me. She looks to be quite agitated," the doctor said. "Come here, miss. Sit down and let me look at you."

Mindy hesitated, but she thought this man may be her best shot. If he could see that she was perfectly fine, he may help her out, or at least let her go. She sat down on the bed and tried to calm herself.

"When did her visions begin?" the doctor asked, turning to Hartthorne.

"Shortly after she came to our house."

"We found them in the woods near the farm. Trespassing," Gargery grumbled. "Her and her brother were up to something."

"We were just passing through," Jasper said, emerging from the corner. "Uh, an aunt—our aunt lives just ten miles over. We were on our way there to get help for my poor sister. If only we could—"

"I'm not his sister. I just need a phone," Mindy pleaded wearily, looking into the eyes of the doctor. They were bloodshot and twitchy, and Mindy could tell that they did not believe her for a second.

The doctor stood up. "Well, I can see nothing physically wrong with her. But her condition as you describe it fits the pattern."

"But you've barely examined her!" Hartthorne protested.

"I've seen enough," the doctor said. "More than enough, really. 'Tis a case of witchcraft, plain and simple."

"Brother Hartthorne, I know this is difficult for you," Gargery said with as much genuine sympathy as he could muster, "but you have to accept the truth in this matter. What's to be done now, Constable Roberts?"

"Well, it seems to me she must be brought before Ann and Mercy."

The minister let out an exasperated sigh.

"Ann and Mercy?" Mindy asked in a weak voice.

The corpulent constable turned his beady eyes on her, "Oh yes, miss. Ann and Mercy have the spectral sight. Their gift has aided the town in a number of these matters already. If the good doctor is right about your condition, Ann and Mercy will tell us who has bewitched you!"

Liar, Liar:

4 Profiles of Accusers from the Salem Witch Trials

Lying can be fun. Annoyed with one of your neighbors? Just accuse her of witchcraft and—poof!—you won't have to see her face around the 'hood anymore! Pretty cool, huh? C'mon, everybody's doing it!

Liar #1: Betty "Baby Spice" Parris

Nine-year-old Betty Parris was prone to bizarre bouts of twitching, twisting, and babbling. Some suggest that her strange behavior was a symptom of the fear and guilt she felt after she and a cousin played at fortune-telling, a practice that was strictly prohibited by the Puritans. Others think she may have had a genuine neurological disorder. Either way, the village doctor was unable to name a medical cause, and he became one of the first to suggest that she was affected by an "evil hand." Coaxed by her reverend father (see Liar #3), Betty eventually accused her housemaid, Tituba, of tormenting her with witchcraft. Around this time, other young girls in Salem began to develop odd proclivities for twitching, twisting, and babbling.

Liar #2: Ann "The Ringleader" Putnam Jr.

Clever and willful, twelve-year-old Ann was the type of child able to tell other girls—even friends who were eighteen and nineteen—what to do. As the girls sat in the courtroom, pretending to be pinched and tormented by spectral apparitions of each defendant, Putnam seemed to be orchestrating the show. Over the course of the Salem witch trials, she claimed to have been afflicted by sixty-two witches in all, and she testified against at least seven of the accused. Fourteen years after the hysteria subsided, Putnam was the only one of the accusers to apologize publicly for her lies. She stood up in church, offered an apology, and then proceeded to take the modern way out: She blamed it all on her late parents.

Liar #3: Reverend Samuel "The Jerk" Parris

It seems just a little too convenient that many, if not most, of those convicted of witchcraft were from families who had clashed with Reverend Parris, the new leader of the Salem Village church. The Salem congregation had hired him the previous year, but many members had misgivings. Reverend Parris not only expected other villagers to cut firewood for his hearth for free, but he demanded that the house he lived in, which belonged to the church, be deeded over to him. He vilified those who opposed him in this, calling them insufficiently godly because they were unwilling to reward

God's minister. Throughout the trials, Reverend Parris fanned the witch hysteria with his sermons, in which he warned that the forces of Satan were at work in the village.

Liar #4: Sarah "The Witch" Churchill

A tragic pattern emerged during the witch trials, wherein the defendants who stood up to their accusers and denied the charges were the most likely to be convicted and hanged. The defendants least likely to feel the noose's tug? Those who admitted they were witches and named others. House servant Sarah Churchill, twenty-five, did exactly that. Perhaps realizing it was the surest way to save her own neck, she sent others—including her employer, George Jacobs—to the gallows. Churchill (sometimes called Churchwell in court records) accused Jacobs of sending his spectral apparition to torment her while his body remained on the other side of a river. Found guilty, Jacobs was executed on August 19, 1692. After the hysteria passed, Churchill admitted she'd lied about it all, especially the part about being a witch herself.

Chapter Eight

Mindy passed out again, and when she finally awoke, she kept her eyes firmly shut. *Please let this nightmare be over,* she thought. She couldn't take it if Jasper or Minister Hartthorne or those insane girls the doctor mentioned—Anne and Mercy—were staring down at her. But she had to do it. She had to find out.

She hesitantly opened her eyes.

Nobody.

The room was devoid of strangers. Unfortunately it was also devoid of her iPod, her television, and her computer. She hadn't awakened from a bad dream. She'd just awakened.

The little bit of brilliant blue sky taunted her through the small window. She'd either slept through the night and into the next day, or it was late afternoon the same day. Either way, she'd have enough time to make it to the highway and flag a ride before nightfall. She hoped.

Mindy listened for the others.

Not a sound.

She carefully propped herself up. She ached from muscles she didn't know she had. Her insides felt like someone was learning to crochet with her small intestines. Whatever Jasper had drugged her with was strong. *All the more reason to get the hell out of this place,* she thought.

Mindy cracked open the diamond-paned lead glass window. A few hogs nosed around along the edge of the yard near the woods, and a couple plucked geese roosted uncomfortably beneath an elm tree, but the garden and the goose-plucking station had been abandoned. She didn't know where Jasper, Minister Hartthorne, and the Walfords were, but despite still feeling like a wrung washcloth, she figured she could make it to the woods.

She climbed out the window and dropped to the ground. The hogs grunted in her general direction.

Mindy froze.

Evidently, they weren't guard hogs because no one came running. She crossed the yard and entered the forest. She padded down the rocky path as quietly as her whooshy skirt and uncomfortable leather shoes would allow.

Well, Mindy thought, *there was one good thing about having absolutely no idea where you were going: Nobody else knew either.* She hoped she was heading in the right direction. She just had to trust her instincts; that's all there was to it.

Behind her, a twig cracked.

Mindy stopped. Holding her breath, she listened.

Nothing, but when she started down the path again, she was certain she heard footsteps behind her.

She picked up her pace. The path connected to what Mindy considered an only slightly larger path, although one that looked a bit more traveled than the one that led away from the Walford farm. Glancing behind her, she turned, thankful when the uneven, irregular path curved and forked. Hopefully whoever was following her wouldn't know which direction she'd gone.

She thought she'd have seen a car or a camper, or at least a convenience store by now, but nothing. Maybe she *had* gone in the wrong direction. If she turned around, she would risk being spotted by whomever was following her. She had to find help, and quick.

The woods thinned and then opened up to a cluster of clapboard buildings. A training field stretched off to her left, and a small private residence sat back from the dirt road a bit. A watchtower loomed across from a three-story clapboard home that looked much like the Walford farm, only maybe a bit larger and fancier with a stable out back and V-shaped molding above the door. On a wooden sign, the word *Ingersoll's* arched over a picture of a tankard of ale. She'd certainly be able to find help in a tavern.

Mindy pushed through the tavern door. "I need to use your phone."

A balding man in his late fifties scratched his head. "My what?"

"I get it, I get it—historical accuracy and all that—but someone is following me, and I need to call the police ASAP."

"We have no *phone* here, and I do not approve of your insolent tone," the tavern keeper said.

Mindy threw her hands up in the air. "Weren't you listening? This is an emergency. Certainly one of you has a cell tucked in a pocket somewhere. Call 911."

A woman, evidently the tavern keeper's wife, took a couple tentative steps toward Mindy. "She speaks gibberish. Perhaps she is ill, Nathaniel."

"I'm not sick, I'm terrified that the crazies who brought me here will find me, and I'm *angry* that you won't help!"

Nathaniel the tavern keeper surveyed her. "I think you're right, Hannah. An evil hand appears to be upon her."

"I've heard enough of this witchcraft nonsense to last three lifetimes," Mindy said. "If you're not going to help me, I'll find someone who will." As Mindy tromped back toward the door, it swung in toward her.

A young boy rushed in, his face ruddy with excitement. "They're bringing Daniel Willard to the pillory!"

Mindy didn't care about the nonsense going on here. She cared about finding a phone. She ducked past the boy.

A crowd of plainly dressed reenactors followed a six-foot square, two-wheeled cart drawn by a single horse.

Surely one of these hundred or so people had bent the rules and brought a cell phone.

The boy came back outside. "Come on!" he said. "If you don't hurry, you'll miss the whipping." He ran off into the crowd.

Mindy's gaze was drawn to the wagon again, and this time she noticed that one person wasn't just following the wagon, he was being dragged behind it, his wrists tied to the tailgate. Behind him stalked a man with a very large whip.

They untied Daniel Willard on a platform in front of a large two-story clapboard building with a stone foundation, inserting his hands and head through holes in a wooden board. It was kind of like the stocks, but the device secured his head and hands instead of his feet.

She didn't care what kind of perversions they were into here. She had to get home. Tapping a stranger on the shoulder, she said, "Excuse me. Can I borrow your cell phone? I need to call 911."

The tall man glared at her. "This is no time for games. It is our duty to witness Daniel Willard's public atonement." He turned away from her and took several steps in the other direction.

CRACK!

Mindy jumped. She turned to see a shirtless Daniel Willard staring penitently into the crowd.

CRACK!

The whip landed again on his bare back, and blood trickled down.

CRACK!

Mindy turned away. "What—why—why are they—?"

CRACK! CRACK!

A serious man next to her said, "He is a liar who cursed his father."

"A repeat offender," the prim woman standing next to him added. "Incorrigible."

That described just about every teenager Mindy knew.

CRACK! CRACK! CRACK! CRACK! CRACK!

The woman nodded. "Daniel Willard would trade a lie for a bit of bread and cheese and a pot of cider."

The whipping stopped. This couldn't be real. No reenactor would voluntarily choose to be whipped—not like that. It had to be some kind of special effect or something.

Cringing, Mindy turned to look.

Blood poured from Daniel's bare back, pooling on the platform at his feet.

It just couldn't be real.

As Mindy watched, a man approached Daniel with a hammer and nails the length of index fingers. He placed the tip of one of the nails against Daniel's left ear and swung the heavy hammer. The nail pierced the hard cartilage of his upper ear and sunk into the wooden pillory.

Then the man took aim at Daniel's other ear.

Mindy felt all the color drain from her face, and her entire body went numb. No reenactment would ever be allowed to do something like that. This was *real*. All this was real.

"What year is it?" Mindy murmured.

"1692, of course," the person next to her said.

"And the place?"

"Do you not know where you are?"

"The place!" Mindy repeated.

"Salem Village."

Mindy felt what little she had in her stomach threaten to come up. She was in the middle of Salem during the infamous witch trials, and the people after her thought she was bewitched.

Law & Order: SPU (Special Puritan Unit):

8 Unusual Crimes and Punishments in Seventeenth-Century New England

Don't do the crime if you can't do the time? Good advice, but in the Massachusetts Bay Colony, lawbreakers faced a lot worse than a stint in prison.

Crime #1: Blasphemy

In crime and punishment, as in everything, the colonial authorities believed that they received their authority from God and that their laws were holy laws. Many criminal statutes were taken right out of the Bible. That's why blasphemy—that is, using the names *God* or *Jesus* in a curse or making fun of religion—was high on the list of criminal offenses. You could actually be hanged for saying things we hear all the time on TV today.

Crime #2: Having fun on Sunday

Puritans took their Sabbath day seriously: It was a day for worship, period. The authorities declared it a crime to shave, make your bed, play sports (good thing football hadn't been invented yet!), or travel on Sundays. Crack a smile in church, and you'd be slapped with a fine. You weren't allowed to cook on Sundays, either, so Puritans had to settle for cold food. And they couldn't enjoy it too much. On Sundays, it was considered sinful to savor food or take too much pleasure from a meal.

Crime #3: Dancing

Like to get your groove on? You'd be out of luck in Puritan New England, where dancing was considered unlawful at all times. Dancing naked in the woods with your friends after signing your name in blood in someone's book would be a particularly bad idea.

Crime #4: PDA

Public displays of affection weren't just frowned upon, they were downright illegal. In 1656, a Boston ship captain arrived home after three years at sea. As he reached his house, his wife came out on the porch to greet him with a hug and a kiss. He was promptly arrested for public lewdness and put in the pillory, a device that locked around the offender's head and hands, and made to stand in public for hours.

Punishment #1: Whipping

The most common punishment in the Massachusetts Bay Colony was a good old-fashioned whipping. A 1648 code of laws limited a whipping to forty lashes, but magistrates could get creative by ordering forty lashes in the public square of Boston, for example, followed by forty lashes in Cambridge, and then move on to more towns. One unfortunate woman who dared preach an unapproved brand of religion was tied to a cart and dragged through the streets of Salem—while being whipped!

Punishment #2: Cutting off ears

Think whipping sounds painful? Wait until you hear about this next punishment. Magistrates often ordered ear amputations for those, such as Quakers, who observed non-Puritan religions, and for a wide range of other offenses. In 1631, Salem resident Phillip Ratcliffe's ears were cut off because he dared to criticize the church publicly.

Punishment #3: Piercing the tongue with a hot iron

Sure, tongue piercings look cool, but the Puritan method of piercing was anything but. As a common punishment for blasphemy, the authorities would grab the tongue with a pair of tongs, pull it out as far as it would go, and then plunge a glowing hot iron through it.

Punishment #4: Branding

Imagine what it felt like to have a red-hot branding iron burn into your forehead. Face-branding was another common punishment in the colony, meted out for a variety of crimes. Burglars got *B*s, drunkards got *D*s, and people who committed vulgar acts got *V*s.

Chapter Nine

For the thousandth time that day, Mindy tried to reassure herself that it was all just a nightmare, that this really couldn't be happening to her, but the blood that dripped from the young man's back and the nails that were driven through his ears said otherwise.

Mindy's mind raced with unanswered questions: How had she gotten here? More important, how was she going to get home? Had Jasper engineered this whole thing? And if he had, why? Why on earth was all of this happening to her?

Then, out of the corner of her eye, she spotted the chiseled profile of Minister Hartthorne. He scanned the thinning crowd intensely. Mindy didn't have to guess whom he was looking for. Her gut had been right when she felt like she'd been followed.

He hadn't noticed her yet, though, or he wouldn't still be looking, so she still had a chance. Without making any sudden motions, she slipped in behind a departing family. From the back, with her white cap and plain olive green woolen skirt and waistcoat, she hoped she looked like every other sated Puritan leaving the scene of an ear-nailing.

A young girl holding her mother's hand glanced back at Mindy. Her mother squeezed her hand in reproach, urging her forward.

"Mumma," the little girl began as the family approached the tavern.

"Hush," her mother scolded.

"But Mumma, there's someone—"

Mindy broke away, willing herself to stay calm and still walk slowly, even without the cover of the family. She needed a place to hide, to figure things out. She couldn't go back into Ingersoll's tavern—too many people. Maybe an outbuilding of some sort.

Then she remembered the stable out behind the tavern. That would do. Being around animals always relaxed her anyhow. If she could just get a couple minutes to breathe, she might be okay.

Glancing behind her to make certain Minister Hartthorne wasn't following, Mindy rounded the side of the stable—and ran directly into Jasper.

Mindy pushed him away. "Get away from me!" she cried, taking a couple of quick steps before Jasper grabbed the back of her skirt.

"Shite, girl! Stop a moment! I'll not hurt yeh!" Jasper hissed. "And I wasn't trying to poison yeh!"

Mindy hesitated. She'd been sure Jasper was up to something, but there was such a note of urgency and sincerity in his voice that she wanted to know what he had to say—maybe she would get some answers at last.

"Sure and we're in grave danger, Mindy." He pulled her toward him, into the doorway to the stable. "We need to talk someplace safe."

Her heart pounding, Mindy allowed herself to be led into the stable. It smelled of hard-run, sweaty horses and hay, but for once these animal smells brought her little comfort.

"Do you want to start telling me what the hell's going on, Mr. Jasper Gordon?" She hissed.

"Shh. Keep yer voice down. We can't get caught in here."

"Why? What would happen?"

Jasper looked embarrassed. "We might get accused of . . . fornication. Another offense worthy of the pillory."

"Yeah, right. *As if* I would do that with *you*. You'd better start talking, mister. Or I am out of here."

Jasper took a deep breath and wiped his forehead. "Stay, girl. Sit. This might take a minute to explain."

"Whenever you're ready."

From his pocket, Jasper pulled out a small glass vial. "I believe you saw me handling this earlier—when I was pouring the cider."

"What is it—drugs?"

"No—not as such, no. But it *is* what that sweaty guy in the black coat back at Pioneer Village wants to get."

"And who is he, exactly? You said you didn't know him."

"Yes, I know I did, but the thing about him is . . . he isn't human."

She laughed. "Yeah, right. What is he, then?"

"The planet Earth is under attack by a race of aliens called Galagians. That kid's name is Andros. He's with them."

"This is not helping."

"Andros is the one who sent us here."

"And here is . . . ?" She still couldn't bring herself to accept it.

"I thought you'd figured that out. Salem Village, 1692."

"Mmmmkay." She paused. "You know, I'm almost afraid to ask this, but why would an alien from another planet send us into the past?"

Jasper held up the tiny vial of colorless liquid, the glass glinting in the light. "It's about this."

Chapter Ten

"This substance . . . it's called *tempose*. It looks a bit like water at first glance, but it's not at all like water or any other liquid in the universe. It's not part of the world of matter in the way water and other fluids are. It exists extratemporally, in past, present, and future at once."

He handed the vial to Mindy, who frowned and held it up to the light. On close inspection, it *didn't* look like water. It shimmered and glittered. It seemed to possess depths that were impossible, given the dimensions of the vial. It differed from water in the way a diamond differs from glass.

"You can see some of its properties just by looking closely, and you're only looking at it in the present—the only way the human sensory apparatus is capable of looking at things. If you could see this from all times at once, you would see every color in the spectrum in it—a vial of glimmering rainbow colors."

"What?" Mindy interrupted with a puzzled expression. "What on earth does that mean—*see this from all times at once*. Who *could* do that?"

"Sure and I'm getting to that part."

"Well, where did this stuff come from? And what does it have to do with what's happening to us?"

"In 1692 it doesn't exist at all—except for the vials I brought here with me. In your time it's exceedingly rare. In the year 2500 it's plentiful. It's produced by the human body—not in your time but once the human race undergoes an evolutionary leap. A mutation in the human gene pool, which probably first occurred soon after your lifetime, led to a slight restructuring of the digestive process. In someone possessing the gene, the pancreas begins to secrete and store tempose. At first this genetic peculiarity was rare, but fairly quickly—in just a few centuries—it sprang up all over the population.

"What's so special about it?"

"In the human body—the human body of the future, I mean—tempose exists in very small amounts, but when it's extracted from many subjects, cultivated, and distilled, it can be ingested. It's possible to artificially elevate a person's levels of tempose. And when it's elevated enough—usually requiring supplements of military-grade strength—tempose permits humans to travel through time.

"Let me give you a brief history lesson. In the twenty-third century, the discovery of this property and the struggle to acquire and exploit tempose for purposes of time travel plunges the world into a state of constant civil war and terror. By the year 2512, the Free Fascist State—a strong, centralized dictatorship—emerges and consolidates its control over the entire globe. The key to its success is its control over the extraction and distillation of tempose. Time travel becomes tightly regulated by the government. Stability and prosperity gradually return, but with it comes a new curse." Jasper paused, shuddering. "It brings *them*. The Galagians."

"That's what Andros is?"

Jasper didn't answer directly. His eyes darkened as he continued. "The Galagians come from a distant and now-defunct planet. For eons, their world was sealed like a cocoon in a heavy cloud layer, and billions of acres of a chrono-kelp grew in this filtered light, support-ing vast seas of photosynthetic, plant-based tempose. This was the medium in which the Galagians lived—a race that evolved outside of time, free to travel between past, present, and future. A partial disintegration of their atmosphere led to their sun's burning off the tempose, which evaporates far more easily than water. Their oceans dried up within a matter of centuries, but by then the Galagians had spread out across the galaxy looking for the substance they need to survive."

"Why do these . . . *Galagians* need it to survive?"

"Sure and it's integral to their very physical makeup. They're tempose-based in the way life on Earth is carbon-based. But there's feck-all more carbon spread about the universe than there is tempose.

"Anyhow, the Galagians arrived on Earth seeking to enslave and farm humanity for its tempose. They wreaked devastation. The human race was completely vulnerable to them when they first appeared because the Galagians can possess the body of any human being who has even only a trace amount of tempose in him. Once inside a human body, the Galagian consumes the tempose until it's gone, and then the invader leaves. A human can live without its tem-pose, but the human race cannot live with parasitic aliens popping into its bodies, taking control, and feeding off it. Worse, the tempose humans produce, even though it is animal-based, has essentially the same chemical structure as botanical tempose, but it's more potent. The Galagians are addicted to it.

"Wait," Mindy interrupted. "They inhabit people's bodies? Don't they have bodies of their own?"

"Sure and they do, but they don't bring them into our atmosphere. They keep them in a ship orbiting Earth, but it's outside of time, where we can't get at it. When they enter our timeline, they enter as spirits, basically."

"What do they look like?" Mindy asked, "Has anyone seen them?"

"To your eyes, looking at them in the present, they would appear as a sort of greenish mist. You can't really focus on them properly if you're rooted to one point in time. Consequently, no human has ever seen them in their true form.

"Anyhow, before too long, the Free Fascist State implemented technologies to screen out the Galagians and prevent them from entering human subjects in the first place. The time police, which were formed initially to regulate time travel and police chrono-crime, were expanded and strengthened and given a new mission: to police the Galagians.

"But the Galagians, who can time-travel, were not so easy to get rid of. Once they were effectively blocked from entering the 2512 human population by chronopolice technology, they simply went back in time to the years when humans produced tempose but before the chronopolice had control. The chronopolice followed them back into the past, and for another decade, we fought a turf war for control of humanity's history.

"Now, the further you go back in time, the fewer humans there are who produced tempose, so the harder it is for the Galagians to hide there from the chronopolice, who stop at nothing to track them down and eradicate them from humans. Major outposts of the chronopolice have been set up in every century going as far back as 2100, but before that time we send only limited patrols back. Genetic historians believe that the mutation first appeared in roughly your lifetime and gradually became more widespread in the gene pool. Before your lifetime, the past is off limits to everyone from the future. The Galagians *can't* go there because there's no tempose, and the humans of the future are forbidden to go there for fear that a disruption to the timeline will weaken the future state. Firewalls have been set up to prevent such travel by the chronopolice."

"So what was he doing in my time?" Mindy asked.

"That's what I'm trying to find out. In case you hadn't figured this out yet, I work for the chronopolice. Not that I'm any great shakes there—they'd never let the likes of *me* into their upper echelons. No, I'm in your time because literally nothing ever happens then, so the patrols are pretty boring. The morning before you and I met, though, I'd received two dispatches from the chronopolice that let me know the shite was hitting the fan.

"The first one was a memo from the intelligence arm of the chronopolice. They're a sort of elite corps and as nasty a gang as you could wish to meet. Their dispatch claimed that the Galagians had developed a truly alarming new device. Supposedly it's a small black sphere—about the size of a marble—that a Galagian can use to enter the body of a non-tempose-producing human. The intelligence people say it's some kind of TAD, or Temporal Accelerating Device— not unlike what the time police use to travel. They're not entirely sure how the Galagians' device works, but presumably it either infuses a human's body with some tempose or somehow allows the Galagian to exist without it. If it's true that they have this, there's a whole world of new bodies they can inhabit between your time and mine— or even earlier."

"Wait—you said that Galagians enter human bodies because of the tempose. Why would they want to inhabit a body that had no tempose?"

"I don't have the answer to that. They may be monkeying around with human history in order to give them some advantage in the future—if the intelligence people are right."

Mindy raised her eyebrows. "Do you have some reason to doubt that this is true?"

"Sure and only the fact that disturbances to the timeline have stayed at a minimum. If they do have this device, they're keeping it under wraps—and that's not normally their style. The second dispatch is a bit more troubling though.

"Just after midnight in the 2547 compound, a Galagian somehow managed to breach security and raid a chronopolice munitions facility. According to the memo, the sergeant-at-arms confirmed that at least one munition was stolen. It was a chronobomb.

"To understand what a chronobomb is, you have to understand what things were like in the early days of the twenty-sixth century, when the Galagians had the upper hand in the war. At that time, a chronotrooper could find himself surrounded by a hundred humans who had all been possessed by Galagians. You could take out your gun and shoot them or throw a conventional grenade, but the humans all die or get blown to bits, and the Galagians run laughing back to their mother ship. Instead, the police used chronobombs. They send out a concentrated pulse of tempose in a fifteen-foot radius, which elevates everyone's tempose levels so sharply that the Galagians are expelled, and the humans retake control of their bodies. As battlefield situations like that became less common, all the chronobombs wound up stockpiled in maximum-security facilities.

"That thing Andros detonated at Pioneer Village? That was the chronobomb. The problem was that he detonated it in a place where it was never intended to be used—your time. If you set one of those things off around humans without natural tempose, it makes them time-travel."

"Is that what happened to me?" Mindy interposed.

"No. It doesn't work like that exactly."

"But—what are you talking about? He detonated it, and here I am, right? I mean, it's a wildly improbable fairy tale to explain what's happening to me, but if you didn't want me to believe it, why did you tell it to me?"

"Well, yes, but if you don't have tempose in you, the chronobomb only sends your spirit or consciousness back—into another body. You came here in your own body—just like me. I'm supposed to be able to time-travel physically. You're not."

"Well, you'll have to excuse me."

"Not at all. I can only surmise that you must have been exposed to tempose at some point recently."

"And all of those other people who were nearby when the thing went off? Chad, Veronica, Serena, Serena's friend Irene—who else, let me see . . ."

"Assuming they are normal, non-tempose-producing humans . . . in your time their bodies are still lying there, unconscious, and their spirits have been sent back in time."

"They're here? With us?"

"I have no idea. There's just no way to—"

Jasper was interrupted by a sharp beeping coming from his pocket. Mindy could see a small red light flashing from under the heavy wool cloth. Jasper pulled out a device that looked like a cross between a Blackberry and an Xbox 360 controller. It was white, substantial, and had a number of buttons across its face and a screen in the middle.

"Ah, excuse me. This is only my bastard chronolyzer," Jasper explained. "A fully sentient automated device that *permits me* to time-travel—thank you very much. It's chock full of useful functions, but it can be a little prickly at times."

Mindy peered over Jasper's shoulder at the green letters scrolling across the screen.

MOST EDIFYING, OFFICER GORDON. ALLOW ME TO OBSERVE THAT YOU HAVE COMMITTED THIRTY-SEVEN SEPARATE BREACHES OF TIME POLICE PROTOCOL SINCE ENTERING THIS BUILDING.

"Yes, I know, but—"

OFFICER GORDON, YOU HAVE PRECIOUS LITTLE TIME AVAILABLE TO YOU. DON'T WASTE IT BY MAKING EXCUSES TO ME. YOUR INFRACTIONS ARE DULY LOGGED AND WILL BE DEALT WITH AT THE APPROPRIATE TIME. I SIMPLY WANTED TO POINT OUT TO YOU THAT YOU ARE WRONG. THERE IS A WAY TO DISCOVER WHERE THE SPIRITS OF THE TWENTY-FIRST-CENTURY SUBJECTS HAVE GONE.

"There is?"

ASK ME.

Jasper frowned. "I bloody well *am* asking you."

BECAUSE I WAS WITHIN THE BLAST RADIUS, MY SENSORS RECORDED FLUCTUATIONS IN THE TEMPOSE LEVELS OF EVERY CUBIC CENTIMETER OF AIR IN A TEN-METER RADIUS.

Mindy interrupted. "So it's true that in the future we use the metric system? Is that because the world is ruled by a fascist dictatorship, or something?" Mindy's comment went unanswered, but Jasper shot her a meaningful look.

THE BLAST PATTERN OF THE TEMPOSE, AND ITS INTERRUPTION BY THE HUMAN SUBJECTS PRESENT, HAS ALLOWED ME TO REPRODUCE A PICTURE OF WHERE EACH PERSON IS AND HIS OR HER RELATIVE PROXIMITY TO THE BLAST AT THE MOMENT OF DETONATION.

Here the words disappeared from the screen, replaced by a green-on-green image like the view through night-vision goggles, or like a photographic negative. Mindy could just make out the outlines of some people—she recognized herself, Serena, Chad, and Veronica in the distance, and in the foreground, a female figure with very skinny arms and a pointy nose, by which Mindy could identify her as Serena's friend Irene. A few other figures looked blurry or were obscured by figures in the foreground.

"Sure and can you tell us where they were sent?" Jasper asked eagerly.

FOR THOSE FARTHEST FROM THE BLAST OR PARTIALLY SHIELDED, THE CALCULATIONS MAY TAKE A WHILE AND MAY YIELD DIFFERENTIAL RESULTS. FOUR I CAN TRACK WITH CERTAINTY.

SUBJECT A: SALEM VILLAGE. DATE: 11.01.1692. LOCAL TIME: 15:47:07.

SUBJECT B: MANASSAS, VIRGINIA. DATE: 07.20.1861. LOCAL TIME 18:37:06.

SUBJECT C: PHILADELPHIA, PENNSYLVANIA. DATE: 05.09.1775. LOCAL TIME: 03:41:27.

SUBJECT D: CHICAGO, ILLINOIS. DATE: 08.24.1894. LOCAL TIME: 07:31:04.

Mindy pointed to the screen. "Subject A—in 1692 Salem, mid-afternoon. Is that me?"

NEGATIVE. The chronolyzer switched back to the green-on-green image and highlighted the skinny, sharp-nosed figure in the foreground.

"Irene? So she's here in 1692 Salem too? But is it true what Jasper said—that I was sent back in my own body because I was exposed to tempose earlier?" Mindy thought for a moment. "Is that why I've been hallucinating?"

NEGATIVE. I HAVE DIAGNOSED MISS GOLD'S AILMENT. THE DIAGNOSIS IS CONVULSIVE ERGOTISM BROUGHT ON BY INGESTION OF INFECTED NATIVE GRAINS.

Mindy raised her eyebrows. "Infected grains?"

BAD BREAD. IN THE TWENTIETH CENTURY, THE ERGOT FUNGUS IS MANIPULATED TO PRODUCE LYSERGIC ACID DIETHYLAMIDE, OR LSD. IN ITS NATIVE FORM, IT POSSESSES MANY OF THE SAME HALLUCINOGENIC CHARACTERISTICS.

"You mean I had . . . what do they call it—a bad trip?"

AFFIRMATIVE.

"What should I do?"

DRINK FLUIDS. AVOID THE BREAD.

Mindy rolled her eyes, struggling to absorb all that she had just been told. "But why did Andros go to the trouble of stealing a . . . chronobomb and sending all of us back in time?"

Jasper answered. "When the spirits of your friends travel back in time, they'll inhabit the bodies of people in the past. The spirits will bring the tempose from the chronobomb along with them, so the Galagians will be able to freely enter those bodies too. They'll be able to travel further back in time than the aliens have ever been able to. Andros has essentially used your contemporaries to provide outposts for the Galagians in the past."

"But why? What are they going to do once they invade our past? You said there's no tempose for them there—why would they be interested?"

"I don't know what they'll do, exactly. Nothing good. They may be trying to attack the chronopolice by changing the course of human history. Who knows?"

"What are you planning to do? Can you get us all back to our own time?"

"Yes—that's the plan. I need to identify the person in each time period who's possessed by a spirit from your time. Then I need to elevate that person's tempose levels gradually—two doses over a twenty-four-hour period should do it. Then I use the TAD inside the chronolyzer to send each one back. With the spirit back in your time, that part of the past should once again be sealed to the Galagians."

"Sounds fairly straightforward . . . I guess."

"Sure and there is a slight obstacle."

"Do tell."

"If Andros or his alien cronies find the body first, they'll inhabit it along with the spirit. The alien will feed on the tempose residue encasing the spirit, and if it consumes all of the tempose, the human from your time won't be recoverable. The human spirit can only exist in this time because of the tempose, just as the alien can only exist by binding to the tempose. If the tempose is gone, the human spirit won't return to its own time—it will be cast into the Void, unable to find its way back."

"Wait—you mean they'll die?"

"Yes, that's what I mean, lass."

"My sister's one of the people we're talking about. I don't know whether to believe you or not—but I want to find her now."

"Yes, I should be able to locate her, but first I have to send you back to safety. If I can find the spirit who went to this place with us—"

"Irene."

"—Yes, Irene. If I can find her, I may be able to apprehend Andros and nip this problem in the bud."

"Fine. But I don't trust you to do this by yourself. I'm coming too."

"No, it's too dangerous—"

The chronolyzer beeped angrily, causing Jasper to jump and

almost drop it on the floor of the stable. Mindy and Jasper looked at the screen.

SINCE YOUR ARRIVAL, YOU HAVE SET IN MOTION A CHAIN OF EVENTS THAT CARRIES A 98.7 PERCENT PROBABILITY OF RESULTANT LETHALITY.

Timeline:

Seasons of the Witch

Salem doesn't have a monopoly on witch-related bloodbaths. A timeline:

2000 BC

One of the first anti-witch laws on record goes into effect. The law, which is part of Babylon's Code of Hammurabi, says that if a man is accused of witchcraft, he has to jump into a river. If he drowns, the accuser gets his house.

1275

In Toulouse, France, a church inquisitor tortures a woman into confessing that she slept with Satan, gave birth to a monster, and fed it the flesh of babies.

1486

The book *Malleus Maleficarum,* or *Hammer of Witches,* a famous manual for witch hunting, is published in Germany. Subsequent editions were published throughout Europe in the sixteen and seventeenth centuries. The book claims that women are more likely than men to be witches.

1581

Beginning in 1581 and lasting until 1593, a series of witch hunts in Trier, Germany, leads to the deaths of dozens or possibly hundreds of town residents. Among those convicted and executed: the town's mayor.

The notorious *Drudenhaus,* or "witch prison," is constructed in Bamberg, Germany, for the purpose of holding and torturing accused witches. Approximately 600 men and women are executed in the town's witch trials.

Salem Village hires the Reverend Samuel Parris as its new minister.

On January 20, Reverend Parris's nine-year-old daughter, Betty, begins having fits and speaking gibberish. Soon, her cousin Abigail Williams and other girls in the village exhibit similarly strange behavior. Parents initially blame video games and hip-hop music before remembering that they haven't yet been invented.

In mid-February, Dr. William Griggs concludes that an "evil hand" has touched Betty Parris.

In late February, Betty Parris, under pressure from her father and others, identifies the family's house slave, Tituba, as her tormentor. She also accuses villagers Sarah Good and Sarah Osborne of witchcraft. The three women are arrested.

Throughout March and April, witchy mayhem ensues. Many villagers are accused, including a pious great-grandmother, a four-year-old girl, and tavern owner John Proctor, whose story will later be dramatized by Arthur Miller in his play *The Crucible.*

On May 27, William Phipps, the Massachusetts Bay Colony's new governor, commissions a new court to try the growing number of accused witches, inspiring a comedy routine later adapted by Abbott and Costello: "What court are you going to?" "Witch court." "Okay, which court are you going to?" "Yes." "But what is the name of the court?" "No, witch is the name." "I just asked you that!" (And so on . . .)

In early June, tavern keeper Bridget Bishop is tried, convicted, sentenced, and hanged on charges of witchcraft. Hers is the first of Salem's nineteen hangings.

Summer: more witchy mayhem, more accusations, more hangings.

On September 22, eight more convicted witches are hanged. These are the final executions resulting from the Salem witch trials.

From October 8 to November 25, Governor Phipps halts further arrests, releases many of the imprisoned, and dissolves the court. A new court, established to try remaining witches, disallows spectral evidence, effectively ending the prosecutions.

Governor Phipps releases most of the prisoners in January for lack of evidence. Before summer, he has pardoned those remaining in jail.

On January 14, the Massachusetts General Court issues a statement of regret over the whole affair.

At the end of the year, Salem Village dismisses Reverend Samuel Parris as its minister.

The Massachusetts General Court declares that the 1692 trials were unlawful.

On August 25, Ann Putnam Jr., one of the chief accusers, publicly apologizes for her role in the events of 1692.

The Massachusetts colonial legislature restores the rights of those accused and offers monetary restitution to surviving heirs.

It's a new century, and witch hysteria once again takes over the nation as *The Wizard of Oz* opens.

The Crucible, a play about the Salem witch trials, opens on Broadway. In it, playwright Arthur Miller draws parallels between the events of 1692 and anticommunist hysteria in his own time.

The Commonwealth of Massachusetts formally apologizes for the events of 1692.

Bewitched, a TV sitcom about Samantha Stephens, a beautiful blond witch married to a mortal advertising executive, debuts on ABC. The show is cursed to be the subject of a terrible film version in 2005.

Sabrina, the Teenage Witch, another TV sitcom about a witch among mortals, debuts on ABC. The title character has a talking cat named Salem, who periodically apologizes for the Salem witch trials.

Chapter Eleven

Jasper spoke up. "I think what the chronolyzer is trying to tell us—"

"Is that we're going to die if we stay here," Mindy finished. "But I'm not cutting and running with my sister stranded in the past. I'm not even leaving Irene stranded here—and I don't even like her."

"The chronolyzer has a point, Mindy." Jasper raised his voice so that Mindy could hear him over the chronolyzer's beeping, which had reached a new pitch of irritability. "This is the height of the witch hysteria in Salem. Everyone suspects everyone else of witchcraft, and outsiders are particularly vulnerable. We're outsiders. You need to get back to your own time. Now." He held out the vial of tempose again. "Drink this, and it should be enough for the chronolyzer to send you back."

"Get that stuff away from me, okay?"

Jasper frowned, his brow wrinkling in perplexity. "The chronolyzer's probably not wrong about this, Mindy. There are a lot of ways to die in 1692 Salem. Neighbor is accusing neighbor of horrible acts of pain, torture, and suffering. When all's said and done, over a hundred fifty people will stand accused, and twenty people will swing on Gallows Hill as witches," Jasper said. "Oh, what is it?" he snapped in exasperation, looking at the chronolyzer.

NINETEEN, the chronolyzer corrected. ONE SUBJECT WAS PRESSED TO DEATH.

"Pressed to death?" Mindy inquired with a shudder.

THE TECHNICAL TERM WAS *PEINE FORTE ET DURE*. ACCORDING TO SEVEN-TEENTH-CENTURY ENGLISH LEGAL PRECEDENT, ANYONE REFUSING TO ENTER A PLEA AND SUBMIT TO A JURY TRIAL WOULD BE SUBJECT TO THIS PENALTY. ACCUSED WITCH GILES COREY REFUSED TO ENTER A PLEA AND BE TRIED, SO HE WAS PLACED BENEATH A BOARD, AND HEAVY ROCKS WERE GRADUALLY PLACED ON TOP OF IT IN AN EFFORT TO MAKE HIM AGREE TO A TRIAL. ROCKS WERE ADDED FOR TWO DAYS, AND COREY SAID NOTHING UNTIL THE END, JUST BEFORE DYING.

"What did he say at the end?" Mindy asked.

MORE WEIGHT.

Mindy's mind suddenly flashed back to her fourth-grade class-room, where one of her classmates—was it Chad?—had painstakingly created a papier-mâché diorama of a person being pressed to death under a pile of rocks while Salem villagers looked on. Apparently the chronolyzer knew history. She looked back down at the still-beeping chronolyzer.

YOU AND OFFICER GORDON WILL SOON BECOME MORE FAMILIAR WITH THE MASSACHUSETTS LEGAL SYSTEM. OFFICER GORDON IS ABOUT TO BE ACCUSED OF WITCHCRAFT.

They looked up, as the stable door burst open with a crash. Several angry-looking, thick-necked men gathered in the doorway, glaring in at them.

"What's this in my stable—*fornicators!*" the closest of the men roared.

"Dammit!" Jasper winced.

"You did sort of see that coming, didn't you?" Mindy whispered.

Colonial Countdown:

10 Terms That Scream "Massachusetts Bay Colony"

Much as the Red Sox, clam chowder, and "pahk yuh cah in Hahvahd Yahd" summon up visions of modern-day Massachusetts, these ten terms evoke the Massachusetts Bay Colony.

Term #10: Spectral evidence

During the Salem witch trials, witnesses often accused witches of tormenting them in the form of evil spirits, or "specters." Crazy as it seems, spectral evidence was accepted as evidence in court and was used to convict many of the town's witches. The courts in Massachusetts eventually ruled that such testimony was a) dumb, b) weird, and c) no longer admissible in criminal trials. The ruling marked the end of witch trials in America.

Term #9: Dominion of New England (1680s)

Call it a super-sized colony. The Dominion of New England was—for a brief few years, at least—a massive administrative district encompassing all of New England, New York, and New Jersey. Its purpose was to impose greater English control over the colonists and to enforce the Navigation Acts.

Colonists, however, would have none of it. Accustomed to running their own government and affairs, they bitterly resented the reorganization and rebelled against their governor. In doing so, they demonstrated the independent-mindedness that would lead to a revolution a century later.

Term #8: Navigation Acts (beginning in 1651)

Passed by the English Parliament between 1651 and 1673, the Navigation Acts were a series of laws imposing tight restrictions on American colonial trade and manufacturing. They required colonists to buy English goods and to ship colonial products via English ports; they also banned manufacturing in the colonies. The colonists were rightly annoyed with the arrangement. They ignored and disobeyed the acts, a show of rebelliousness that prefigured the American independence movement.

Term #7: Halfway Covenant (1662)

It's a story as old as time: Children grow up and rebel against their parents. In mid-seventeenth-century New England, youngsters were unwilling to focus their lives completely on religion, as their parents and grandparents had. In response, the Puritan clergy offered them a watered-down version of church membership called the Halfway Covenant, which allowed colonists to become church members without meeting rigorous standards of knowledge and behavior. Passage of the covenant signaled the arrival of a younger, hipper Massachusetts, one that was evolving away from its stodgy Puritan beginnings.

Term #6: Middle Passage

Imagine being crammed into a belowdecks hold with a ceiling so low that sitting up, much less standing, was impossible. Imagine being forced to lie on a hard, wooden floor next to hundreds of other people chained hand and foot, each person folded against the next like stacks of spoons on their sides. Imagine suffering through rampant disease and watching the people around you die in droves. That's what life was like for slaves on the Middle Passage, the cruel voyage of a slave ship from the west coast of Africa to the New World. Today, the Middle Passage is a symbol of the cruel and dehumanizing nature of slavery.

Term #5: Triangular trade (seventeenth century)

This triangular pattern of international trade had a three-stop route: 1) A ship departed from Europe and sailed to Africa, where it traded goods for slaves; 2) the ship sailed to the Caribbean, where it traded slaves for goods like molasses and rum; and 3) the ship sailed back to Europe or to New England with its new bounty. In the triangular trade, human beings were treated as cargo, the same as molasses and other goods.

Term #4: Salutary neglect (about 1650–1750)

England interfered with its American colonies as little as possible between 1650 and 1750 (with some notable exceptions—see Term #9). This period of salutary neglect allowed the colonies to establish their own legal, political, and economic systems, giving them a tantalizing taste of independence.

Term #3: City upon a Hill

No, it doesn't refer to San Francisco. "City upon a Hill" was the humble nickname that Puritan leader John Winthrop gave America in his famous sermon "A Model of Christian Charity." The metaphor introduced the concept of American exceptionalism—the idea that America could be a unique society held to a higher moral standard than the rest of the world (Ha! Whoa, ho, man. Heh, sheesh. Gimme a sec . . . well, yes, anyway). The speech was so inspirational and eloquently phrased that many presidents have cribbed from it in their own speeches.

Term #2: Separatists (seventeenth century)

Separatists believed that the Church of England, England's official state religion, was too corrupt to be reformed and that the only option was to separate from it entirely. Separatists led the Pilgrims, who founded the Plymouth Colony in 1620.

Term #1: Puritans (seventeenth century)

Like the Separatists, Puritans believed that the Church of England was rife with problems. However, instead of splitting from the church entirely, they decided the state religion just needed to be "purified" (hence their name). The Puritans followed the Pilgrims to the New World, where they founded the Massachusetts Bay Colony. Today, many feel that the streaks of conservatism in American culture can be traced back to our Puritan roots.

Chapter Twelve

"I think we've uncovered something worse than fornication." The man who spoke, a burly, gray-haired figure who looked to be about fifty years old, stepped past the owner of the stable. Behind them, peering anxiously into the stable, stood Minister Hartthorne, who spoke next.

"And what would that be, Sheriff Corwin?"

"Can it be any plainer, man? 'Tis witchcraft, to a certainty."

Mindy gasped.

"It does not seem so certain to me," rejoined Hartthorne. The other men eyed him with irritation. "On what evidence do you make this claim?"

"Do you know these two, Minister Hartthorne?" asked Sheriff Corwin.

"They are visitors to Salem. Gargery Walford and I have offered them our hospitality. Common decency demands we be careful of what we accuse them. I say again: What evidence do you have of witchcraft?"

As Hartthorne spoke, Jasper tried to slip the tempose vial into Mindy's hand. "Mindy, this could be your last chance," he whispered. "Drink the tempose and let me send you home!"

"Stop that!" Sheriff Corwin's voice boomed out. "Step away from each other." He grabbed the vial out of Mindy's limp hand. "*This* is the evidence—this potion."

"No!" Mindy said. "It's not like—"

"Jasper Gordon," Sheriff Corwin said, his small, dark eyes narrowing, "you are under suspicion of having committed sundry acts of witchcraft, doing much hurt and injury unto the bodies of Ann Putnam, Mercy Lewis, and . . . this young woman."

Two henchmen, who had entered the stable behind Hartthorne, hauled Jasper up by his elbows.

"And what's this?" Sheriff Corwin said, plucking the chronolyzer from Jasper's grasp. The screen read, SHALL I TRANSPORT YOU TO SAFETY, OFFICER GORDON?

"It is the devil's book!" Sheriff Corwin exclaimed.

The chronolyzer's screen turned black.

"Jasper Gordon, you are accused and are hereby ordered to withstand examination tomorrow at ten o'clock in the forenoon under suspicion of witchcraft," Sheriff Corwin said.

"You can't do this!" Mindy yelled.

Jasper shook his head at her urgently. "Don't try to intervene, Mindy. Do as they say. I'll trust my innocence to the court."

Sheriff Corwin frowned. "I believe she is in league with this wizard."

Hartthorne spoke up. "No. Do not send this girl to prison. She has been ill. She is . . . not in her right mind. We do not know that she has been bewitched. Again, I say that I have offered her my hospitality. I . . . I have seen her suffer, but I believe she's done no harm."

"She must at the very least appear in court to give witness. If I let her go, she may slip out of town to wherever she came from." Sheriff Corwin paused a moment. "The jail is full to bursting. It is unfortunate for her she has no relative in the village to stay with on bond."

Hartthorne contemplated this for a moment, sighed, and then said quietly, "I will take her back to my sister's farm. I will be the court's surety that she will appear in the meetinghouse as required at the next session."

Sheriff Corwin scowled. "So be it, then. I remand her into your care. See that she appears at the appointed time." He turned to go, signaling to his henchmen.

"Stay a moment, Sheriff Corwin," Minister Hartthorne said. "If you have no use for them, may I take the potion and the device with me as well?"

"Why?"

"In the hope that careful study may reveal something about the affliction that plagues this girl and the others."

Corwin's small dark eyes narrowed. "They are evidence of his wizardry. They must be presented to the court."

"I will bring them. You may rely on it."

With a grunt, Sheriff Corwin handed Hartthorne the tempose and the chronolyzer and walked away with his henchmen and Jasper. Hartthorne pocketed the items. Mindy watched Jasper until Hartthorne took her by the arm and led her out into the late afternoon sunlight. They walked away from the cluster of buildings and back onto the path leading to Gargery's farm. They walked on a moment in silence.

Mindy found the silence increasingly uncomfortable. After a moment, she stopped.

"I'm not crazy, you know."

"No doubt. I didn't say—"

"You did! Just now. I *am* in my right mind."

"I meant no harm. Back at the farm this morning—"

"Yes, I was sick, okay? I'm better now."

"I am glad." The minister was silent a moment, and they began to walk again. "What you said when you first came here—about our *acting* . . ."

"Look I get it, okay? You really are a minister. I understand."

"Why would you doubt it?"

Mindy looked up at him. "It's hard to explain. I guess where I'm from, clergymen aren't usually so . . . young. Or something. Anyway, what I need now is a lawyer. To get my brother out of jail."

"You seemed afraid of him before. I believe you denied he was your brother."

"I told you, I was sick. I didn't know what I was saying. I'm fine now."

They walked on for a few moments. Finally, Hartthorne said hesitantly, "Do you think it *could* be that someone or something was afflicting you?"

"You mean like a witch? No. I think I ate something that was bad for me. It made me sick for a while, and now I'm better. Look, do you think you could take me to where they're taking Jasper? Do they have visiting hours at the jail or something?"

"We will not be able to gain access today. Look, we're here."

As they exited the woods and entered the farmyard, Mindy could see that something was horribly, terribly wrong. Large piles of feathers dotted the grass, but as they approached the first pile, Mindy could make out a head, neck, and webbed feet.

Although part of her still remembered her hallucination too vividly, Mindy couldn't let her anxiety keep her from helping an animal. She knelt down to examine the goose.

"It's dead," she said. "And so are all these others, it seems." Even the geese that Mindy saw get plucked naked earlier were lying on their sides, their necks at contorted, odd angles.

Gargery came from the barn with a wooden shovel. He glared at them. "Me geese have died! It is witchcraft, pure and simple. Jonathan, you can't bring her here, carrying death and destruction in her wake. Death, destruction, *and rocks!*" he muttered, although Mindy could not tell whether this last phrase was truly an accusation against her or just one of the farmer's general-purpose epithets.

"Brother Gargery, she is sick," protested Hartthorne. "She is in my care. She is my responsibility this night."

"Arr—I'll not have witchcraft in my house. Be she witch or be'n't she—she's bad luck."

Mindy ventured to speak, in what she hoped would be a placating tone. "I think your geese ate bad bread. I would throw it away if I were you."

"Throw it away!" the farmer screamed. "Nonsense! I'll eat rocks before I throw my good bread away."

This was too much. Mindy began to tear up. She tried to choke back the tears, but they ran down her hot, flushed cheeks anyway. She had tried to be strong for Serena, but now the last door in Salem was apparently closed to her. She was going to have to go to prison.

Colonial Countdown Part Two:

10 People Who Rocked the Massachusetts Bay Colony

The Pope of Geneva, the protofeminist, and other interesting Massachusetts Bay peeps.

#10: Sir Edmund Andros (1637–1714)

London-born Andros was appointed by the English to serve as colonial governor of New York and, later, the Dominion of New England—a short-lived (1685–1690) super-colony that encompassed the Massachusetts Bay and Plymouth colonies. Hired to impose tighter control over the colonists, he tried to enforce laws on a society that had been largely self-governing for more than half a century. After King James II of England was overthrown on that side of the Atlantic, the colonists tossed Andros in prison in 1689, a move that foreshadowed the revolutionary events of the next century.

#9: Metacom, a.k.a. Philip of Pokanoket (c.1590–1661)

The son and successor of Pilgrim-friendly Massasoit (see #3), Metacom was originally given the European name "Philip" as a gesture of camaraderie with the colonists. While Massasoit's tribe lived peacefully with the English, Philip's tribe wasn't so fortunate. After attempting to resist further westward expansion by the colonists, Metacom found himself embroiled in a tragic conflict—later called King Philip's War—which devastated his people, killing 3,000 Native Americans and reducing entire subtribes to handfuls of starving refugees. The colonists triumphed over Metacom and put his head on the end of a pole in celebration. It was displayed in Plymouth for twenty-five years.

#8: Anne Hutchinson (1591–1643)

A self-styled Boston preacher who dared to challenge Puritan orthodoxy, Hutchinson is now considered a pioneer of both religious and women's rights. She spoke out publicly about her beliefs and, in an era in which women were supposed to be obedient to men, criticized the Puritan patriarchy. In 1637, Governor John Winthrop (see #1) condemned her preaching as a "thing not tolerable . . . nor fitting for [her] sex." Several years after she was banished from the Massachusetts Bay Colony, Hutchinson and members of her family were killed by hostile Native Americans. Some Puritans thought God's wrath had led to Hutchinson's violent death.

#7: Roger Williams (c.1603–83)

As minister of the Salem church, Williams preached the concept of separation of church and state, an idea that was blasphemous to most of his fellow Puritans. One of the first true advocates of religious freedom in the colonies, he argued in 1634 that civil magistrates had no authority to enforce religious laws. However, Massachusetts governor John Winthrop so vehemently

disagreed that he banished Williams from the colony. In 1638, Williams up
and founded the colony of Rhode Island and the city of Providence.

#6: Increase Mather (1639–1723)

An influential Boston clergyman, author, educator, and statesman, Mather
expressed doubts about the evidence in the Salem witch trials. He argued
that "spectral evidence"—a victim's testimony about an attack by a specter,
or spirit, that physically resembled the suspect—was unreliable. Mather's
doubts helped turn public opinion against the trials and end them. Increase's
son, Cotton, was not such a calming influence as his father. Cotton published
Memorable Providences Relating to Witchcrafts and Possessions, his
observations of witchcraft at work, which effectively contributed to the witch-
hunt hysteria in Salem.

#5: John Calvin (1509–1564)

Calvin, a French clergyman, was the big cheese in the Puritan movement.
Both the Pilgrims and the Puritans came to America so they could follow
Calvin's no-frills, back-to-the-Bible brand of Christianity without being
persecuted for it. The word *Calvinism* means roughly the same thing as
Puritanism. Calvin was such a powerful preacher in his adopted hometown
of Geneva, Switzerland, that he virtually took over the city and shut down all
the fun stuff, including theaters, music halls, and brothels. He was mockingly
called the "pope of Geneva."

#4: Squanto (c.1580s–1622)

A member of the Pawtuxet tribe, the English-speaking Squanto (whose real
name was Tisquantum) served as translator for the Wampanoag and the
English settlers. After spending several years as a slave in England, Squanto
escaped back to the New World in 1619, only to find his entire tribe wiped

out by smallpox. He lived among the Pokanoket tribe and taught the Pilgrims how to grow corn and perform other tasks essential for survival.

#3: Massasoit (c. 1590 – 1661)

Massasoit was the chief of the Pokanoket tribe of Native Americans and leader of the Wampanoag confederacy of tribes. His friendship and cooperation with the Pilgrims allowed the Plymouth Colony to survive its difficult early years. In 1621, he joined with the Pilgrims, ushering in a peaceful alliance that lasted until after his death. When Massasoit was seriously ill during the winter of 1623, one of the Pilgrim leaders, Edward Winslow, personally fed the chief a duck broth seasoned with strawberry leaves and sassafras that helped him regain his strength.

#2: William Bradford (1590 – 1657)

A Pilgrim leader who served as governor of the Plymouth Colony for thirty years, Bradford shaped American society by organizing the colony under principles of community self-government and individual self-reliance. He was the main author of the Mayflower Compact of 1620, a voluntary agreement between the colonists to abide by the laws of the new society.

#1: John Winthrop (1588 – 1649)

Winthrop was a Puritan leader who served as founding governor of the Massachusetts Bay Colony. He established the colony as a network of tightly organized towns with a degree of self-determination—a model for American civic government. His famous sermon, titled "The City on a Hill," depicts the Puritan colony as an exceptional society defined by its special relationship with God. Several U.S. presidents have quoted this sermon in their own speeches.

Chapter Thirteen

"Brother Gargery, calm yourself," said Minister Hartthorne. "We can seek shelter at the ordinary." His voice had a calming effect on the farmer and on Mindy. He made it seem like things were not quite so bad after all.

Then he did something very unexpected. He put his arm around Mindy and, turning her back around toward the village, led her gently back down the path. It was a simple gesture, but it was the first truly kind thing Mindy could remember seeing anyone do in Salem Village. She tried to choke back her emotions once more so that the minister wouldn't see them. When she realized that he was resolutely looking on ahead, giving her time to collect herself, the tightness in her throat relaxed a bit, and she began to breathe more easily.

Mindy soon learned that *ordinary* was some kind of Puritan-speak for tavern. The two of them returned to the village, and Minister Hartthorne engaged rooms for each of them, with a minimum of fuss, at an inn belonging to one Nathaniel Ingersoll. Hartthorne also arranged for food, which Mindy was afraid to eat after the hallucinations she'd endured earlier in the day. But she had no choice—she was famished. She pushed her bread to the side but tore into the stew served in a trencher—a hollowed-out wooden board that served as a plate—focusing on the root vegetables and picking around the meat. When her hunger had been sated a bit, she looked up at Hartthorne. He was smiling back at her with kind eyes, clearly impressed at how much she had eaten.

Mindy found the courage to meet his eyes and said, with a quaver in her voice, "You don't think I killed your brother-in-law's geese, do you?"

"No," Hartthorne scoffed, but he looked troubled nonetheless.

"No?" She frowned. "You don't look sure."

"It isn't the geese. It's just—this place didn't used to be like this." He let out a breath and looked at her.

"What did it used to be like?"

"We were in it together. Life was hard, but we shared one faith, and we helped each other on." He gestured with his arm, indicating the town outside the inn. "I can't even count how many of these houses I helped build, from the time I was big enough to hoist a beam or lift a stone.

"Now, forty-eight people are already in Corwin's prison house. It grows and grows. People go into it, but no one ever comes out of it."

"Why? What happened to Salem?"

Hartthorne gave her a quizzical look, as if trying to figure her out. "Salem Village, indeed the entire Massachusetts Bay Colony, is suffering through turbulent times—as you must know. Many say that we have failed as a community, and these witch trials are the result. Here in Salem, we Congregationalists have a covenant with God that transcends king and country. When bad things befall someone in our small community, we tend to see it as God's judgment on our moral failings."

He lowered his voice and leaned in across the table so that his shoulder-length brown hair fell forward. "Many in the colony believe we are on the brink of the End of Days, that we are experiencing

God's final battle. They quote Matthew 24:24: 'For there shall arise false Christs, and false prophets, and shall see great signs and wonders; insomuch that, if possible, they deceive the very elect.'"

Mindy shuddered. "And what do you say?"

"I say that the elect are indeed being deceived . . . but not by witches." His voice became softer. "I believe that many of the girls who claim to be afflicted are actually lying. Many others are of my opinion, but no one will raise his voice against what is happening." He frowned. "You, however, did not seem to be faking anything today. You seemed genuinely afflicted by something."

"Something I ate."

"There may well be a natural explanation for what is going on. I intend to watch the court proceedings and find it out, if I can." He leaned forward and spoke with conviction. "I believe there are reasons for things that we don't know. I believe the villagers act out of fear—not because they know the truth. I trust the evidence of my senses and my reason."

"That doesn't sound very minister-like." Mindy winced at her own thoughtlessness. "I didn't mean—"

Hartthorne colored. "We should take our rest now. I'll show you to your room."

That night, Mindy lay in her tiny room, pondering the enigma that was the minister. When she'd first arrived in the past, he had struck her as so un-minister-like because of his romance-novel good looks. She had thought his costume badly done, the ever-present Bible a clichéd touch. So it turns out he really *was* a minister. That really *was* a Bible. She would have to be on her guard around him. Despite his free-thinking views, his religion made him as liable to throw in with the witch hunters as not, in her opinion. She certainly didn't remember reading about any conscientious objectors among the Salem clergy in her history lessons.

The chronolyzer could tell her what to do next—assuming she could get her hands on it and figure out how it worked. She had already resolved to try to break into Hartthorne's room and steal it once the household was asleep.

Mindy took the lamp from her room, shielded it so it released the smallest possible amount of light, then tiptoed silently to Minister Hartthorne's door and listened. His breathing was soft and regular. Carefully she pushed his door open. She stood still for a moment, waiting to see if the dim light roused the minister. If she only knew where Minister Hartthorne had stashed the chronolyzer.

A soft glow emanated from beneath a stack of papers on the night stand.

As she slipped the chronolyzer beneath her waistcoat, she wondered if the little electronic device was psychic as well as sentient. She turned and padded toward the door.

Minister Hartthorne turned over in the bed.

She froze. Then, when he didn't move again, she slowly pivoted on her heel and took a step toward the door. But in the dark, she knocked something over, and Minister Hartthorne leapt up with a start.

Chapter Fourteen

"Mindy, is that you?"

"Um, have I been . . . sleepwalking . . . *again?*" Mindy winced in embarrassment at her palpable lie.

The minister frowned. "Do you know what people would say if they caught you here?"

"Yes, fornication, the pillory—I'm starting to catch on." Salem was beginning to remind Mindy of summer camp. She'd just been caught sneaking into the boy's dorm.

"So why *are* you here?"

While trying to think of an answer, Mindy shifted the shield on the lamp to shed a bit more light, then she reached down to pick up the object she'd knocked over. It was the minister's book.

"Answer me, Mindy."

As she picked it up, something fell out of the book, and she saw that it was pressed leaves and flowers held between the pages. She opened the book and saw that its pages were blank and filled with meticulous drawings of plants, insects, animals, and other natural objects.

"Hey, this isn't a Bible after all!" *These are amazing,* she was about to add, but Hartthorne cut her off.

Although there was little light, she saw his face flush. "That book is mine! You have no right to take it."

"Does everyone else know this isn't a Bible?" Mindy asked, then she wished she could take it back. Why did she always put her foot in her mouth like this?

"Mindy, I—please, just put my book back down there and go back to bed." He watched in anger as she did as she was told.

As soon as the door closed, the chronolyzer lit up. THAT WAS VERY STEALTHY, the chronolyzer displayed. WOULD YOU BE INTERESTED IN A POSITION THAT RECENTLY OPENED UP WITH THE CHRONOPOLICE?

"Really?"

NO. YOU'RE ABOUT AS SMOOTH AS FARMER GARGERY'S FIELDS.

"You saw me with Minister Hartthorne?"

OF COURSE.

"But you're just a machine."

I AM A FULLY SENTIENT ELECTRONIC ASSISTANT WITH COMPLETE SENSORY CAPABILITIES.

"So if you have complete sensory capabilities, what does this room smell like?"

DIRT, HEADCHEESE, AND ALE.

Unfortunately, the chronolyzer was correct. "All right, then. So you can smell."

I CAN ALSO TRANSPORT YOU TO THE FUTURE IF YOU DRINK THAT VIAL OF TEMPOSE.

"But what about Jasper? He's going to be tried as a witch tomorrow."

WIZARD, BUT THAT'S NOT THE POINT. IF I TRANSPORT US BACK TO JASPER'S TIME IN 2512, I CAN NOTIFY HIS SUPERIOR DEWITT, WHO CAN SEND A CHRONOPOLICE INTELLIGENCE OFFICER TO RESCUE HIM. THESE EXTRICATIONS ARE COMPLICATED AFFAIRS. WE MUST BE VERY CAREFUL NOT TO DIVERT THE TIME STREAM.

"There's not much point in arguing about it, since I *can't* do what you ask."

WHY NOT?

"I didn't take the tempose vial—just you."

So go back and get it.

"There's no way I'll be able to sneak into Minister Hartthorne's room twice."

Technically you didn't sneak into his room once. You were caught.

"Technically, I sneaked in, but I didn't sneak out, smart-ass."

You must obtain that vial of tempose and drink it as quickly as possible. Andros is addicted to tempose. Whoever has the vial is an easy target for him.

"So here's a question, then. From what I've seen of Salem, it's the very last place I'd ever choose to hang out if I were an alien. Plus, it's low on tempose, right? What on earth does Andros want in Salem?"

He's looking for one of his Galagian colleagues, whom he thinks has been transported from their mother ship into the same body that your friend Irene was sent into. He's been using his temporal accelerating device to pop in and out of people all over the village, checking them for traces of tempose and making them behave oddly for his private amusement.

Mindy rolled her eyes, not even trying to conceal the sarcasm in her voice. "Are you trying to tell me an *alien* caused the Salem witch trials?"

Andros may have contributed to the spread of the hysteria, but it's generally believed that there was some initiating incident, perhaps an illness brought on by ergotism or encephalitis, that was interpreted as witchcraft and subsequently used by "the afflicted," as well as the rest of the village, to resolve longstanding, festering disputes, many of them concerning conflicts over land.

"In English?"

Here ye, here ye! Let it be known that—

"And now without sounding like you walked out of a renaissance fair . . . please?"

You said you wanted it in English.

"I meant I wanted you to explain it in normal terms, Robo-geek."

Oh, you mean in terms a seventeen-year-old, twenty-first-century teen could understand.

"Exactly."

So are words with two syllables okay, or should I stick to monosyllables?

"Hey, you're a nasty little phone, aren't you?"

You know, if I didn't want to get back home and into the hands of a competent operator, I really wouldn't bother.

Mindy glared at the chronolyzer.

I see that.

"Good."

If you're going to be hostile—

"Just get over yourself and go on."

The big thing that caused the trials—Oops! There I go with two syllables again!

"You think you're being funny. You're not."

I'm programmed to be funny. Perhaps I need an upgrade. In the interim, I'll try to stop . . .

Here the words disappeared from the screen, replaced by the single word Loading . . . Then, after a brief pause, the machine resumed.

. . . giving you grief—that is the early twenty-first-century idiomatic expression, I believe.

"That would be nice. I already have a minister, a bunch of irate villagers, and, evidently, an alien giving me a hard time. I don't need to add you to the list."

THE CONGREGATIONALISTS, WHICH IS WHAT THE PURITANS CALLED THEM-
SELVES, WERE BOTH VERY RELIGIOUS AND LITIGIOUS. MANY EVENTS LACKED
OBVIOUS EXPLANATION, SO, FOR EXAMPLE, WHEN A CHILD GOT SICK FROM EATING
BAD BREAD OR BEING BITTEN BY A DISEASE-CAUSING MOSQUITO, THEY LOOKED TO
RELIGION AND THE COURT SYSTEM FOR AN ANSWER.

BIZARRE BEHAVIORS AND UNEXPLAINED ILLNESSES WERE THEREFORE THE
PRODUCT OF WITCHCRAFT, AND THE WITCH HAD TO BE FERRETED OUT AS THE
BIBLE COMMANDED AND THEN TRIED FOR HER CRIME AS THE LAWS OF THE
MASSACHUSETTS BAY COLONY REQUIRED.

THE WITCHCRAFT TRIALS OF 1692 WERE SEIZED UPON BY SOME OF THE COLO-
NISTS AS A WAY OF SETTLING GRIEVANCES OVER LAND AND PROPERTY THAT HAD
BEEN SIMMERING FOR YEARS. SOME FAMILIES APPEAR TO HAVE AIRED THEIR GRIEV-
ANCES BY ACCUSING THEIR NEIGHBORS OF WITCHCRAFT.

"Friendly folks, these Puritans," Mindy said, sighing. "Nice, hon-
est, Christian folk."

The chronolyzer ignored her sarcasm. Perhaps it was programmed only to deliver it, not receive it.

MANY OF THE AFFLICTED GIRLS' INITIAL FITS WERE PROBABLY THE PRODUCT
OF REAL ILLNESS, LIKE YOURS. HOWEVER, IN A SOCIETY WHERE GIRLS LACKED
CONTROL OVER THEIR OWN ENVIRONMENT, THEY MAY HAVE LEARNED TO ENJOY THE
POWER THAT CAME ALONG WITH THE ACCUSATIONS AND SUBSEQUENT TRIALS AND
BEGAN FAKING FITS TO EXERT CONTROL OVER THEIR WORLD.

Mindy's brain reeled. The whole scenario brought to mind the play
The Crucible, which she had read in tenth grade, and the countless
Salem history lessons she had endured every year since elementary
school. "So Jasper's going to trial tomorrow because a bunch of girls
are faking symptoms to get attention?"

ESSENTIALLY.

"So all I have to do is tell them I made a mistake when I said he wasn't really my brother and that he was insane and trying to poison me, that I take it all back and that the girls are lying. They'll have to let Jasper go, and then we can all go home."

I WOULDN'T RECANT IF I WERE YOU. THAT CAN ONLY TURN OUT BADLY. MARY WARREN DID THAT AND—

Mindy powered the chronolyzer off. "I have had enough of you and your pessimistic, didactic lectures. I'm going to take care of this myself."

The chronolyzer turned itself back on. I'M WARNING YOU. IF YOU RECANT, IT WILL END UP WORSE THAN YOU CAN POSSIBLY IMAGINE. BUT SUIT YOURSELF. IT'S YOUR NECK THAT'LL STRETCH ON GALLOWS HILL. AND *DIDACTIC?* GOOD WORD.

The screen went blank.

Salem's Most Wanted:

7 Profiles of Accused Salem Witches

In Salem, most of the villagers accused of witchcraft defied the stereotype of the warty, pointy-hat-wearing witch. Among those accused were a cute little girl, a churchgoing great-grandmother, and several men. Here's a small selection of the more than 185 accused during the Salem witch trials. Not one of them had green skin.

Witch #1: Tituba (Verdict: Guilty!)

Just as a small match lights a huge fire, the Salem hysteria started in a single household. Samuel Parris, the Puritan minister of Salem, couldn't figure out what was wrong with his nine-year-old daughter Elizabeth (known as Betty), who was having fits and behaving strangely. She threw herself on the floor, twisted her legs and torso into painful-looking postures, uttered unintelligible noises, and—perhaps most alarming to her father—covered her ears during his sermons. Parris suspected that his Caribbean house slave, Tituba, who was probably of mixed Native American and African heritage, was involved. He accused Tituba of witchcraft. It's thought that he may have beaten her to gain a confession. Tituba blamed other villagers for drawing her into witchcraft, thus setting into motion the accusations, lies, and all-around hysteria that would continue for the next year.

Witch #2: Bridget Bishop (Fate: Death by hanging!)

Bridget Bishop was a bit too racy for Salem tastes. She tended bar at her husband's tavern, and neighbors gossiped about her loud voice. During one memorable argument, she even shouted at her husband in public. Bridget had also been known to laugh out loud in public, something that respectable Puritan women were not supposed to do. Worst of all, she dressed to accentuate her figure. Historical accounts mention in particular a dress with a tight red bodice that came to a point above a black skirt. Unlike Tituba, Bridget vigorously denied being a witch, pointing out that she was a member in good standing of the Puritan Church. The court quickly found her guilty, and an eager crowd gathered to watch her hang on June 10, only eight days after she was charged.

Witch #3: John Proctor (Fate: Death by hanging!)

Honesty was a dangerous policy during the witch trials, as the case of John Proctor proves. Proctor, a successful farmer and tavern owner, had a reputation for speaking his mind, and he did not hesitate to do so as the witch trials began. He thought the accusations were all nonsense, and while others surely agreed, Proctor made the mistake of voicing his opinion in public when his wife Elizabeth was arrested and charged with witchcraft. Proctor became the first of many men to be accused, and after being tried and convicted, he became the first of six men to be executed.

Witch #4: Sarah Good (Fate: Death by hanging!)

Life was not good to Sarah Good. Her father, an innkeeper, committed suicide when Sarah was seventeen. Her mother's second husband took control of the father's considerable estate, and poor Sarah received no inheritance. By the time she was an adult, she was homeless and destitute, reduced to begging house to house for food and shelter. Other villagers found her an unpleasant nuisance, and she developed a reputation for being sullen and spiteful. Probably because she was so disliked, she was among the first accused of being a witch and tried in June of 1692. Sarah's husband William testified against her. Pregnant when convicted, Sarah gave birth in jail, only to see the baby die. She was hanged on July 19, 1692.

Witch #5: Dorothy Good (Verdict: Not guilty!)

Four-year-old Dorothy Good (some accounts give her age as six) was the daughter of Sarah and William Good. One of the accusers apparently coaxed this little girl into testifying against her mother before the trial magistrates. Instead of simply accusing her mother, however, little Dorothy told the judges that she herself was a witch. It's likely that she did this because she desperately wanted to be with her mother. She spent eight months in jail but—unlike her mother—was not hanged.

Witch #6: Rebecca Nurse (Verdict: Not guilty! On second thought . . . guilty!)

Many Salem residents began to realize that something was seriously wrong when Rebecca Nurse, a well-liked, seventy-one-year-old great-grandmother and pious church member, was arrested as a witch. Despite the danger of confronting the court, prominent citizens stood up in defense of their elderly neighbor. One petition extolling Mrs. Nurse's impeccable virtue and piety bore the signatures of thirty-nine of Salem's most respected community leaders. And in fact, the jury actually returned the unheard-of verdict of "not guilty." But Rebecca's good luck turned out to be short-lived. Upon hearing the verdict, the young women who were the chief accusers began to shake and cry out as if tormented by Mrs. Nurse's evil magic, prompting the judge to challenge the verdict. The trial was reopened, and the jury eventually found her guilty. A few days later, her church excommunicated her, and on July 19, 1692, she was hanged.

Witch #7: Giles Corey (Fate: Death by . . . well, you'll have to read it for yourself!)

Eighty-year-old Giles Corey, accused of witchcraft by a family servant, was less concerned about losing his life than about losing the property he had acquired over the course of his long career as a farmer. He knew that if he was convicted, his property would be seized, leaving nothing for his heirs. He also knew that under English common law, the court could not convict him if it could not try him, and it could not try him unless he entered a plea. When Corey refused to enter a plea, court officials resorted to a positively medieval method to get him to change his mind. They had him stripped naked and laid on the ground with a stout board on top of him. Then heavy rocks were piled on the board, one after the other, but Corey still refused to enter a plea. Eventually, he was crushed to death. Reportedly, his last words were "More weight." Although he died a terrible death, Corey succeeded in saving his property for his heirs.

Chapter Fifteen

"I have some bad news," Minister Hartthorne said the next morning as he and Mindy walked the several hundred feet to the meetinghouse for Jasper's preliminary examination. He looked at her carefully.

"What?" Mindy asked, dreading the answer. She couldn't handle another bit of bad news—but she pretty much knew what he was going to say anyway.

"The device that was found on your brother Jasper has vanished."

Mindy swallowed hard. She didn't meet his gaze. "Really?"

"This will not be good for Jasper. The magistrates will think he spirited away the evidence against him."

"But nobody can make things just disappear."

Hartthorne's tone was flat and serious. "Unless the device reappears, the magistrates will view its disappearance as evidence of witchcraft."

"I suppose so."

She knew he thought she took it, and she didn't want to lie, but she needed the chronolyzer to get back home. Besides, once she told the judges that it was all a misunderstanding, they'd have to forget the whole thing—she hoped. If they had the chronolyzer, though, they might think its technologically advanced properties were magical, and Jasper still might be accused. *Better to have missing evidence than incriminating evidence,* she thought.

"Of course, this won't help him much either." Minister Hartthorne held up the vial of tempose. It was now half-empty. "What is this liquid that he was trying to make you drink? What does it do?"

"It doesn't do anything. It's just water."

Minister Hartthorne sighed. "You don't trust me to do the right thing, do you?"

"It's just water," she repeated, unable to raise her gaze to meet his.

Inside the meetinghouse, people crammed into the tall-sided pews and onto the benches in the balcony. Others stood crowded together in the back. Although the windows had been thrown open, the austere, dim interior radiated heat and buzzed with flies and mosquitoes. The chatter of endless suppositions quieted down a bit as Minister Hartthorne led Mindy to a bench in front of the pews. She took her seat next to the other afflicted girls. From the conversations around her she gathered the names of two of the girls—Ann Putnam and Mercy Lewis. Mindy sat nearest to Ann, who had her thin arms folded at her chest, her thin lips pursed in a tight smile, and her hard eyes directed at the courtroom. Mercy Lewis, the heavy-set one, looked bored and uncomfortable and was sweating profusely. The other girls were new to Mindy. They ranged in age from maybe twelve to nineteen or twenty. Ann was the youngest.

Mindy scanned the room for Jasper, but she didn't see him. In the front of the room beneath the pulpit, two men sat behind a large wooden table. They both looked very serious, though the older man in his sixties seemed the most rigid. The younger man had sharp features and keen, intelligent eyes. Off to the side, another man sat with paper and quill, evidently preparing to take notes.

Despite the warmth in the room, Mindy found herself shivering. Mercy Lewis was sneaking looks at Mindy out of the corner of her eye, but when Mindy turned to meet Mercy's gaze, the other girl looked away, seeming irritated. A bead of sweat dripped off of Mercy's chin.

The memory of words she'd heard popped into Mindy's head. *Don't even talk to me about Mercy. I don't even want to discuss Mercy.* The sudden realization of who she was looking at made Mindy sit up with a snap and burst out, "It's you . . . Andros!"

Fortunately, amid the chatter and gossip in the courtroom, no one seemed to be paying attention to them.

"You narced on me after all." Mercy's voice was quiet, her breathing heavy.

"I didn't!"

"I don't suppose you'd consider giving me that vial, would you?" Mercy sighed and looked down with a frown, as if she wanted to throw up. "This would all be so much easier then." She looked up at Mindy. "And I can pretty much guarantee your fascist friend won't hang today. Don't worry: The chrononarc has more. He's probably planning to leave you here, you know. Something to do with preserving the precious time-stream balance. I could take you back, though."

Mindy didn't bother to point out that she didn't have the vial. "You can go to hell!" she snapped.

This was not a popular remark in the courtroom. A number of spectators turned to glare at Mindy seriously.

"Where's Irene?" Mindy hissed.

Mercy shifted uncomfortably in her chair, her face flushed. "She ran out of tempose late last night."

What was it Jasper had said would happen once the tempose was gone? *They go to the Void.*

Mindy was incredulous. "You *killed* her?" she whispered.

"Her spirit went to the Void, yes. Which is where you're going to go if you can't talk your way out of this trial. You need me."

Suddenly Mercy's eyes rolled back in her head, and she appeared to faint. Mindy's head started to throb. She could feel her blood pounding and an overwhelming feeling of pressure inside her head.

Mindy struggled to shut Andros out of her mind. Her face felt flushed, and she broke out into a sweat. She cried out, causing most of those seated in the courtroom to look over at her. Some even stood up to get a better view.

"Silence!" a deep, magisterial voice boomed out. The elder magistrate rose to his feet, and the meetinghouse instantly quieted. "Bailiff!" he intoned. "Bring the court to order."

Early Arrivals:

5 Groups Who Got to North America Before the Pilgrims Did

We were here first! No, we were here first! No, we were here first! No, we were . . .

Group #1: Stone Age Europeans (Estimated Time of Arrival: perhaps 19,000 BC)

Some archeologists believe that ancient flint spear points found in several places throughout the Americas—including a site in Virginia—are so much like others found in Spain and France that the people who made the tools must have been related. The theory is that a group of Stone Age Europeans may have brought their tool-making skills with them across the Atlantic. And how did they manage an ocean crossing? Using small kayaklike watercrafts, the early explorers would have followed the edge of pack ice—similar to the polar ice cap—that spanned the ocean during the Ice Age. Hunting and fishing along the way, they would have traveled short distances at a time on a trip that would have taken decades.

Group #2: Asians from Siberia (Estimated Time of Arrival: perhaps 10,500 BC)

Most experts believe that the major migration route into North America was across a massive land bridge called Beringia that once connected Alaska to northeastern Asia. Until recently, the most widely accepted theory was that all Native Americans are descendents of a single group of Asian hunters who followed migrating game animals into the New World. More recently, many scientists have changed their minds because of evidence that Native Americans are more diverse in terms of language groups and DNA than was previously thought. Newer theories envision different groups of people crossing from Asia into America over a period of many thousands of years.

Group #3: Vikings (Estimated Time of Arrival: around 1000 AD)

He didn't keep a ship's log, so it's hard to say for certain how much of North America Leif Eriksson visited around the year 1000. A Norwegian who had settled in Greenland, this famous seafarer led the first of what might have been several expeditions to the coast of Canada. The fact that these sailors set foot in America was established by archeologists who in 1960 found ruins of a Norse settlement on the island of Newfoundland. Among the items the Vikings left behind were butternuts, which are American walnuts that don't grow that far north. This means the Norse likely sailed farther south—but how far south is anybody's guess. Some scholars think they sailed past Cape Cod before turning around and heading home.

Group #4: John Cabot and his crew (Estimated Time of Arrival: 1490s)

You might say that sea captain John Cabot is the original international man of mystery. He might have been born in Genoa, Italy, but nobody's sure. He might have been lost at sea in 1499 on his second voyage to North America for his adopted country, England. Yet there's a chance that he or one of his crew saw New England and made it back to Europe. Around this same time, a map was drawn by a Spaniard. The map's depiction of Cape Cod and other features of the North American coast must have been based on firsthand knowledge.

Group #5: Other Europeans (Estimated Time of Arrival: 1500s to 1619)

Although the Pilgrims were early European settlers in America, they weren't the first in North America or even in New England. The first post-Viking European settlement on the continent was Spanish. They founded Saint Augustine, Florida, in 1565. The first successful English settlement in North America was Jamestown, Virginia, founded in 1607. Earlier European settlements in New England were either intentionally temporary—such as a Dutch outpost in Connecticut before 1620—or failures, such as a poorly planned English colony in Maine that lasted less than a year in 1607. The *Mayflower* crowd deserves kudos as the first to establish a successful, permanent European settlement in New England.

Chapter Sixteen

As quickly as it had come, the feeling of being invaded was gone. Mindy slumped weakly in her chair, panting to catch her breath.

At the magistrate's command, a familiar rustic figure rose to his feet with self-important slowness, scanning the courtroom with a scowl. It was farmer Gargery Walford.

"Neighbors. Farmers. Goodwives." Gargery gestured toward the court expansively. "You know well why we are come to this court of law on this day."

The magistrate, a portly figure in a white wig and velvet gown, glowered uncomfortably. Leaning toward farmer Gargery, he said in a low but resonant voice. "A simple 'All rise' would be sufficient, bailiff."

Gargery raised his voice louder. "Neighbors, good neighbors. You know why we are here today—and what's more, you know *me*. Right well you know me." Here he looked at the court meaningfully. "Full many of ye were with me when we raised the roof beam on my farmhouse three year ago."

A few scattered murmurs of "Aye, aye" were heard in the courtroom. The magistrate looked up at the ceiling.

"Some of ye even labored beside me pulling rocks out of the cold, hard ground on the stony fields the Lord saw fit to give me in his wisdom—though not quite so many of you," he added bitterly.

"Bailiff!" barked the magistrate impatiently.

Gargery cleared his throat loudly, then continued. "The magistrate sits today in public examination of these duly convicted sorcerers, as you well know."

"Bailiff, sit down. No one has been con—"

"Once the convicted are arraigned," continued Gargery calmly, "they must go before the court of Oyer and Terminer. Oyer and Terminer, I say. 'Tis *to hear* and *to determine*." He cocked his head meaningfully. "Now ye yourselves shall hear, and ye yourselves shall determine—of this!"

Farmer Gargery pulled a large and very heavy object out of the satchel at his feet. It was a rock—about thirty pounds, from the look of it, encrusted in moss and fresh soil. It looked as if it had been dug out of the ground that morning.

Farmer Gargery slammed the rock down onto the table in front of the magistrate, as the courtroom gasped. Dirt clods, clumps of moss, and fine, dark silt sprayed all over the table, the papers on the table, and the magistrate, who sputtered with rage.

"*This*—" Gargery indicated the rock with his finger. "This stone broke my plow this very morning. 'Twas me new plow, the one neighbor Joseph sold to me for a spotted pig only this August last. 'Twas hitched to my best pony—now practically lamed from the shock of plow and rock colliding."

The magistrate stared up at the farmer in outraged disbelief. "What is the meaning of this? Bailiff, remove this rock from the court immediately."

"'Tis witchcraft!" thundered Gargery. "Witchcraft—plain as this stone sits on this table. If it could be plainer I don't know how."

"Bailiff, I warn you—"

"I think I've made me point," said Gargery with satisfaction, snatching his dirty rock from the table. "This community has been sorely tried—and there's more of it to come, sure enough. No one is safe. No one!" he repeated, for the court's benefit, before sitting down with his rock.

The magistrate shook his head in exasperation. "Bring in the accused," he muttered.

Jasper hobbled down the aisle, his delicate hands bound and feet in shackles, Sheriff Corwin towering over him on one side and a constable towering over him on the other.

Andros, having abandoned Mindy, proceeded to body-hop through the afflicted girls, each one passing out as he moved on to the next. Ann awoke on the floor, disoriented. When Mercy awoke and spotted Jasper before the magistrates, she threw herself about, convulsing. Suddenly Ann was doing the same.

A woman in the pew behind Mindy whispered, "See how the wizard afflicts them all, just by entering the meetinghouse?"

"What are you people—retarded?" Mindy snapped back at her.

This was not good.

Jasper took his place in front of the magistrates at the table. He had put on a brave face, but his clothes were wrinkled and his hair fell in sweaty bangs across his forehead. He looked like he had had a hard night in prison. He smiled weakly at Mindy and winked, but the usual sparkle in his eye was a bit dimmed, and the smile did not reassure her.

The magistrate spoke. "I am Magistrate Stoughton. Jasper Gordon, you are accused here for acting witchcraft upon Ann Putnam, Mercy Lewis, and Mindy Gold. What do you say to this you are charged with?"

"I am not guilty."

The girls fell down in grievous fits, writhing and twisting. Ann acted as if she were being choked.

Mercy Lewis held up her hand. A pin was stuck into it. "Jasper Gordon did this to me!"

"Look there," Magistrate Stoughton said, "she accuseth you to your face. Is it not true?"

"No," Jasper said. "Sure and I've been standing here the entire time. How would I be able to stick a pin in a girl from this far away?"

"You are acting witchcraft upon their bodies."

"But I'm not a witch," Jasper said matter-of-factly.

"That you were found hiding from the authorities in a stable is an acknowledgement of guilt, but yet not withstanding, we require you to confess the truth in this matter."

"I wasn't hiding. I was trying to find Mindy."

Minister Hartthorne stood up. "It is true. Mindy Gold's affliction caused her to flee the farm without cause. The same has happened to many of the other unfortunates during their afflictions."

"I am not a witch," Jasper repeated.

"Can you pray the Lord's Prayer, then? Let us hear you."

Jasper paused, then stammered, "Em, well, I've never been too much of a Holy Joe, but let's see . . . The Lord is my shepherd—"

"That is the twenty-third psalm!" the magistrate thundered.

The audience whirred at the scandal.

"Em . . ."

Minister Hartthorne whispered, "Remember, it begins, 'Our Father which art in heaven.'"

"Right. Noted." Jasper shifted from one foot to the other. "Our Father which art in heaven . . . yellowed be thy dame. United Kingdom come—"

Another uproar from the audience.

"Do you see that God will not suffer a wizard to pray to him?"

said the magistrate, furrowing his brow so that his bushy eyebrows shook. "You are guilty. Confess."

Jasper said nothing.

Magistrate Stoughton said, "If you desire mercy from God, then confess and give glory to God."

Jasper still did not respond.

The magistrate wiped his brow with a handkerchief. "We will now hear testimony that bears on this case."

Sheriff Corwin stepped forward. "I found this man hiding in Ingersoll's stable. He must have been communing with the devil."

Ann nodded. "At that very moment he was sending his apparition to torment me!"

"Your spectral sight is as clear as always, Ann Putnam," Magistrate Stoughton said.

Mindy couldn't believe it. Why were they taking this twelve-year-old girl's word for something nobody else even saw?

"Be there any more testimony?" Magistrate Stoughton asked.

Mindy stood up. The room stilled. Jasper sent her a warning glance, but she ignored it. She had to stop this nonsense. "This has all been a huge mistake. Jasper Gordon is no witch. While I stayed at the Walford's farm, I ate bread that made me sick. While I was sick, I saw many things that did not make sense and said many things that I did not mean. I take it all back. Jasper is not a witch."

Ann Putnam stood up. "She is in league with him! When he entered the meetinghouse, he did sorely afflict us, but he did not harm Mindy. And now she defends him! Mindy Gold is most certainly a witch herself!"

I'll Get You, My Pretty:

8 Evil Powers Attributed to Salem's Witches

Can't find your keys? Is your cow not producing milk? Don't get mad—blame the witch down the street!

Power #1: Flying

Let's say one villager's saddle has gone missing, and at the same time, another villager has mysteriously lost a wad of cash. Villagers could pin both occurrences on the same suspected witch by citing her ability to fly. Then, as now, witches were thought to ride aboard broomsticks. They were also suspected of harnessing the power of tornadoes for transportation, giving those broomsticks a supercharged boost.

Power #2: Stealing a cow's milk by sticking a knife into a wall

If a farmer's cow went dry—that is, stopped giving milk—it was a serious misfortune. In seventeenth-century New England, no one knew anything about the infectious agents that can cause a cow to dry up. Many people believed that a witch could "milk a knife" by sticking a knife in a wall and then coaxing the milk out of the knife handle and into a bucket.

The milk was thought to fly invisibly through the air from the cow's udder to the knife.

Power #3: Sending a demon to steal valuables

Witches were thought to have help from a *familiar,* a demon that took the form of a cat or a rabbit. The witch would send his or her little demon buddy into a neighbor's house, where it could eavesdrop on private conversations, steal, or otherwise make mischief. Familiars were believed to drink blood from their witch partners by sucking on the skin, leaving a mark that looked like a bruise but was thought to be a "witch's teat." Suspected witches were sometimes stripped and inspected for stray bruises, which were taken as proof of guilt.

Power #4: Killing with a toad's breath

In seventeenth-century New England, toads were widely considered evil little critters and witches' consorts. In fact, it was believed that a witch could commit murder simply by sending a toad to breathe on the victim, as the animal's breath was thought to contain deadly poison. Even a dead toad was thought to be dangerous. The witch could burn the remains and save the ashes, which were thought to be useful in many potions. One pamphlet from the 1600s suggested that nothing was more dangerous than toad ash mixed with the powdered bones of dead Christians.

Power #5: Creating fatal illness by burning a voodoo doll

Back in the days before over-the-counter fever-reducers, many people associated fevers with the fires of Hell. Witches supposedly learned how to inflict fatal fevers on their innocent neighbors from the big guy, Satan himself. The technique? They used a *poppet,* the seventeenth-century version of what we think of as a voodoo doll. According to the belief, the witch would fashion a miniature model of the victim out of a root, a lump of clay or wax, or even a cornstalk. He or she would then cook or burn the poppet, and as the fire charred and consumed it, the person it represented would fall into a fever leading to death.

Power #6: Changing into an animal or another person

Arrr, when you put on your pirate costume next Halloween, keep in mind that the costume tradition is rooted in folklore about witches. Witches were thought to be able to take on the shape of an animal or a trusted friend or family member. They shape-shifted by stealing a personal item, such as an article of clothing, from the person whose shape they wanted to take. The Halloween tradition is a reference to this uniquely witchy power.

Power #7: Brewing potions

It may be a cliché, but witches really were thought to brew up magic potions. The ingredients in a typical witch's concoction may have included crystals, animal parts, and many kinds of plants, ranging from healing herbs to deadly poisons. In fact, many of today's common names for herbs and other plants—including St. John's Wort, monkshood, henbane, and foxglove—were supposedly coined by medieval folk-healers who were considered witches in their day. In the 1600s, many people believed that witches' brews could kill or heal, depending on the ingredients. It was not uncommon for someone in England or colonial America to seek out a witch in search of a cure for an illness or for something to ward off evil.

Power #8: Disappearing

Unlike Harry Potter, witches didn't need a magic cloak to become invisible. Instead, all they had to do was whip up a potion of sow thistle sap and toad spit (sounds delicious!). Like shape-shifting, this ability was another way for witches to sneak around undetected and cause mayhem.

Chapter Seventeen

"You're a liar!" Mindy shouted. She turned to the magistrates. "The reason I didn't fall down on the floor like a two-year-old having a tantrum when Jasper came in is that he didn't do anything to anyone! These girls are faking their fits and making up stories to get attention."

Minister Hartthorne stood up again. "Mindy is no witch. If anything, she was afflicted as the others are."

The girls threw themselves into fits once more. "Her specter bites me!" Mercy said.

"Please do not pinch me so, Mindy Gold!" Ann cried.

"I'm not doing anything!" Mindy said. She couldn't believe this. By telling the truth to try to help Jasper, she'd gotten herself accused as well. Andros had to be behind this. Maybe he was possessing the girls to make them speak out against Mindy. Not that she could share her theory with anyone without further proving she was a witch. She was in so much trouble.

Magistrate Stoughton pointed at two strong men near the front pews. "Bring Mercy Lewis to the wizard Jasper and make him lay hands on her."

The two men carried Mercy over; she flailed and twisted the entire way. Sheriff Corwin grabbed Jasper by the hand and made him touch Mercy's arm.

Suddenly, Mercy's fits ceased.

Mindy stood up. "Hey, that's closer to proof that she's lying than proof that she's afflicted. If Jasper was a wizard, why would he cure this girl if it made it look like he was a wizard?"

Mercy grew wide-eyed. She stared at the cross-beams in the ceiling and then pointed at something invisible up above. "There! Mindy's apparition sits up in the rafters, suckling a yellow bird betwixt her fingers!"

"Jasper hurts me!" Ann said. "Last night he brought his book to me and would have me write in it."

"I understand we have that book," Magistrate Stoughton said. "Bring it forth."

Minister Hartthorne said, "It has vanished."

"The devil would not have his book looked upon by gospel folk," Magistrate Stoughton said, nodding.

Sheriff Corwin said, "When we apprehended the wizard, he was trying to make Mindy drink a potion. We left it in the custody of Minister Hartthorne. Has the wizard caused that to vanish as well?"

All eyes turned toward Minister Hartthorne, who stepped forward to stand directly in front of the magistrates. Tall and proud, and certain in his conviction, he said, "I have the vial of liquid. I do not know why they had it, but do I know it to be no potion." He held up the vial.

Magistrate Stoughton said, "How do you come by this knowledge?"

"Last night I drank some of the liquid. I felt no malefic effects from it."

Another flurry of shocked whispers swept the crowd.

"He's right," Mindy said. "The liquid is only water. I will drink it down right now, in front of all of you, to prove that it does no harm."

Before anyone could stop her, Mindy took the vial and downed the contents.

Suddenly the man in the front left pew fainted. Andros was back to checking out the villagers for his body-hopping friends.

The man next to the man who fainted gave Mindy an odd, lopsided grin, then passed out. Like dominoes, the parishioners collapsed one after the other until the entire congregation either lay passed out or was waking up disoriented.

"She has bewitched us all!" a woman cried.

Suddenly a board flew from the back of the room, narrowly missing an elderly woman.

Mindy scanned the room. The last person still conscious in the very back smiled at her before passing out. Mindy knew she was the only person who had seen what Andros had done.

"The witch is bringing down the meetinghouse!" someone shouted.

"She will kill us all!" another villager said.

The crowd surged toward the exit, a tumble of arms and legs fleeing the oppressive heat of the dimly lit meetinghouse. Some people helped those who were still unconscious from Andros's body-hopping, but others simply stampeded over the prone bodies.

The constables started hauling Jasper toward the door, but his bound hands and shackles made progress so slow that Sheriff Corwin and his assistant became more concerned about their own safety than Jasper's security and left him in the turmoil.

Jasper struggled to stay upright amid the crush of bodies—most of them larger than his—but finally fell to the floor.

Mindy rushed over and pulled him under a vacated pew.

"We've got to get out of here," Jasper said. "But we need the chronolyzer before we can transport back to our own times. Do you know what happened to it?"

"I stole it from Minister Hartthorne's room last night."

"Fair deuce, Mindy! Now give it to me, and I'll begin the transport calculations."

"No," Mindy said.

"And why not, girl? D'ye want to hang?"

"We can't leave without Minister Hartthorne. You saw how these people are. If we magically disappear after he defended us, he'll be the next one accused."

"Well, we can't take that hunk with us. Time travel requires high levels of tempose administered in doses over time. You just drank the last of the tempose, and even if you hadn't, we couldn't give him enough right now to allow him to travel with us. You've got to forget him, Mindy. He's on his own."

"Jonathan Hartthorne didn't leave us on our own. He stood up for us, when no one else would! *You* didn't even stand up for yourself. When they caught us in the barn, you just went with them without a fight."

"There were too many of them. If I fought back, you would have helped me try to escape, and then you would have spent the night in shackles in the Salem Village watch house too."

Mindy softened. "You were trying to protect me?"

"Right—and a holy show I made of it at that."

"Well, thank you," Mindy said quietly, suddenly aware of just how close their bodies were, wedged in the space beneath the pew like they were. She could feel Jasper's breath against her cheek.

He avoided her eyes. "Well, one of us had to stay out of the pokey if we were going to get out of here. Of course you went and messed that all up by getting yourself accused of witchcraft."

Mindy snorted. "I didn't do anything but try to save you! It was those stupid girls. I think Andros may have possessed them and made them say those things."

"I didn't see any indicators of possession in the afflicted girls after Andros passed through them. I think they're just doing what they've been doing for the last six months—picking up on cues and making up the most dramatic story they can.

"The situation here in Salem Village is way out of our control, Mindy. We simply need to transport home and hope for the best for Minister Hartthorne."

"I won't leave without him, and you won't leave without the chronolyzer, so I figure you'd better come up with solution."

"Well . . . there is one other way. Based on a statistical analysis of the accused, afflicted, and executed, I do see one other thing we might do to garner ourselves some time."

"What is it?"

"Confess."

Suddenly Mindy felt a hand grab her foot and drag her out from beneath the pew.

Chapter Eighteen

"Mindy, are you intact?" Minister Hartthorne asked. "Did he harm you?"

"I'm fine, I'm fine," Mindy said, standing up and brushing off her long skirt.

Minister Hartthorne called to Sheriff Corwin. "The prisoner is here!"

As the parishioners cautiously filed back in, Sheriff Corwin hauled both Mindy and Jasper to the front of the meetinghouse.

"Not Mindy," Minister Hartthorne said. "Just Jasper."

Magistrate Stoughton scowled. "She has been accused, just as her wizard has been. She must stand with him."

As Mindy waited for the rest of the audience to be seated, she agonized over Jasper's solution. Confess? What good would that do? Was he just trying to get rid of her so that he could return home? But she had the chronolyzer, so he couldn't go anywhere without her. It didn't make any sense.

Mindy glanced over at Jasper. He mouthed, *Trust me.*

"I know you are not a witch," Minister Hartthorne said to her. "I will see that you are cleared of these vicious accusations."

Swallowing hard, Mindy said, "No need for that. I'm about to confess."

Minister Hartthorne stepped backward. "You're going to do what?"

"I confess," Mindy said louder. "I am a witch."

"Right. And so am I—only more so," Jasper added.

The crowd settled into silence. She imagined that this was the best entertainment they'd ever gotten. Well, if they wanted a story, she was going to give them one.

"I . . ." she was suddenly very conscious of the congregation's eyes on her. "I am a witch. Plain and simple. I come from a long line of witches, a proud heritage. One day we plan to open a witchcraft shop in the village."

A collective gasp of shock and horror went up in the courtroom.

"Oh, we'll probably make most of our money off soap and candles, things like that. And T-shirts, don't forget the T-shirts. Black and orange with cats all bunched up—"

"Sure and we met the devil in the forest two nights ago, did we not, Mindy?" volunteered Jasper.

"Right! And he—he gave us rocks to plant in the fields."

"He made us sign his book. We danced naked in the moonlight."

"Right. Naked. *Buck* naked."

The congregation hung on every word.

Magistrate Stoughton turned to Minister Hartthorne. "That you defended them would seem to indicate that you, too, are a wizard."

The afflicted girls launched into their now-familiar fits, accusing Minister Hartthorne of pinching, pricking, and biting them, even choking them to the point that they couldn't speak.

"I am falsely accused," Minister Hartthorne said. "Your worships, all of you think this is true?"

"What do you think?" Magistrate Stoughton asked.

"I am as innocent as the child born tonight." Sweat poured down Hartthorne's brow. He clenched and unclenched his fists.

Ann acted as if she were being choked.

Mercy cried, "With each movement of his hand, he afflicts her!"

Minister Hartthorne wiped his sweaty palms on his breeches. "I do no such thing."

Ann pounded her thigh. "He puts pins in my leg!"

Minister Hartthorne glanced toward the bench of afflicted girls, and they all fell to the floor in fits.

"You see? You look upon them and they fall down."

"It is false. The devil is a liar."

"Why do you afflict these girls?"

"What would you have me say? I never wronged any man in word nor deed," Minister Hartthorne said.

"Can you look upon these girls and not knock them down?"

"They will dissemble if I look upon them."

"How far have you complied with Satan, whereby he takes this advantage against you?"

"Sir, I never complied but prayed against him all my days. I have no compliance with Satan in this. What would you have me do?"

"Confess if you be guilty."

"I will stand in the truth of Christ. I know nothing of this." Minister Hartthorne stood proud and defiant.

A very sweaty old woman from the village got to her feet, swaying uncomfortably. "See if his *Bible* really be the Lord's book. Mayhap it is some devilry."

All eyes turned toward Hartthorne, who blushed. Sheriff Corwin snatched the black book from Hartthorne's hands and opened it. Pressed leaves and flowers fell out of it. Corwin held the book open for all to see.

"It contains nought of the word of God! 'Tis not written in at all— just these drawings of plants and birds and creeping insects."

Shouts went up around the court. "They are the wizard's familiars!" "Recipes for his diabolical potions!"

Magistrate Stoughton sighed. "The truth is clear to all. You are all three ordered away to be bound hand and foot to await trial at the Salem Town jail."

Sheriff Corwin loaded Mindy, Hartthorne, and Jasper into the small horse-drawn cart to transport them to jail. They bound Mindy's hands in front of her but left her feet free.

"Why did you tell me to confess?" Mindy whispered to Jasper as Sheriff Corwin started the cart jolting down the road.

"Well, statistically speaking, it was the correct thing to do. No accused witch who confessed during the trials was hung."

"It's still getting us sent to jail," Mindy said.

Minister Hartthorne eyed Jasper critically. "How do you know so much of future events? Are you indeed a wizard?"

Jasper ignored him. "It got us away from as many prying eyes as possible. Now we can use the chronolyzer to transport out of here."

"I told you, no. Even if it's only the cart driver who sees us magically disappear, we're still leaving Minister Hartthorne behind. He'll hang for certain."

Jasper leaned in closer to Mindy. "So we'll escape first—all three of us. Minister Hartthorne can flee to safety until the trials are over, and everyone will assume we did too."

"I don't know." With some maneuvering, Mindy reached beneath her olive waistcoat and pulled out the chronolyzer. "Chronolyzer, were you listening?"

ALWAYS. UNLESS I'M BUSY.

"Will Jasper's plan work, or is he just making stuff up so he can get home?"

It will work. A significant portion of the suspected witches escaped jail or left town before examinations. In October, spectral evidence—i.e., the fits and claims of invisible apparitions—will no longer be allowed into evidence.

Even if he did manage to get himself accused between now and then, in May of next year, Governor Phipps will pardon everyone still in jail or with outstanding warrants. In 1752, witchcraft will no longer be allowed to be prosecuted as a crime. Minister Hartthorne should be fine.

"Okay then," Mindy said. "Let's figure out how we're going to escape."

The cart jolted to a stop, the horse whickering uneasily. Sheriff Corwin turned around. His face was red and dripping with sweat as he turned one big, red, glistening eye upon them. "Oh, I don't think you'll be doing that," he said.

"*Andros!*" Mindy cried.

Number Crunching:

14 Stats About the Colonies

Who says math is too hard? In this list, we really do a number on U.S. history.

0 survivors of the first English colony in the New World

When explorer John White returned to Roanoke Island in North Carolina in 1590 after being away for three years, he discovered that the English settlement was completely deserted. To this day, nobody knows what happened to the 150 settlers.

11 ships in the Winthrop Fleet

Unlike the *Mayflower,* which sailed solo, a well-organized flotilla of ships transported the Puritans who founded the communities around Boston harbor. It was called the Winthrop Fleet after the Puritan's leader, John Winthrop.

19 lifeless bodies hanging from the gallows

In addition to all of those who were convicted and executed on charges of witchcraft in Salem, more than 175 men and women were imprisoned, and one man was crushed to death when he refused to acknowledge the charges.

20 slaves sold in Jamestown, Virginia

In 1619, the very first shipment of African slaves arrived in the United States aboard a Dutch ship. The number of slaves in the United States would eventually peak at nearly four million.

35 years in the average lifespan

In seventeenth-century America, more than two out of every ten children born died before reaching age ten. However, if you made it to the teen years, you had a reasonable chance of seeing age fifty, and some people lived well into their eighties and nineties.

41 signatures on the Mayflower Compact

All of the male passengers aboard the *Mayflower* signed this famous agreement to abide by the laws of the new colony. Signed as the ship lay at anchor in Provincetown Harbor, the Mayflower Compact is considered an early indicator of democratic tendencies among the new Americans.

50 survivors of the first winter in Plymouth

The *Mayflower*'s passengers faced a long and difficult winter when they first settled in their new home. Less than half of the colonists and ship's crew survived until the spring of 1621; the rest died of scurvy, pneumonia, tuberculosis, or a combination of those ailments.

90 feet from stem to stern

The *Mayflower,* a typical seventeenth-century sailing vessel, was about as long as the distance of the base path between home plate and first base on a full-size baseball diamond. The ship was about thirty feet wide, or the depth of the goal on a football field.

102 passengers aboard the *Mayflower*

The Pilgrims had planned on bringing ninety-one people, but their second, smaller ship, the *Treadwell,* dropped out of the expedition. Of the *Treadwell*'s thirty passengers, eleven joined the *Mayflower* party, and the rest stayed behind in England.

300 dollars (take that, Donald Trump!)

In 1626, the Dutch colonist Peter Minuit traded sixty Dutch guilders' worth of hatchets, blankets, and other goods to Native Americans in exchange for the entire island of Manhattan. Converted into today's dollars, that's about how much you'd pay for a new iPod!

5,000 early New Yorkers

Today, the New York metropolitan area is home to well over eight million people. In 1700, the Dutch trading outpost was America's second biggest colonial city, with a remarkably cosmopolitan population of 5,000.

7,000 early Bostonians

In 1700, Boston was North America's largest city (today, it's the 24th largest U.S. city, right behind #23, Seattle).

275,000 early Americans

My, how we've grown since 1700. According to the 2000 census, the total U.S. population has now surpassed 300 million.

500,000,000 people (total!)

Sure, it sounds like a lot, but the estimated population worldwide in 1650 is just a tiny fraction of the estimated number of people in the world today—6.5 billion and increasing at a faster rate every year.

Chapter Nineteen

Sheriff Corwin, whom Andros had possessed, turned around and sat backward on the driver's seat. "There will be no escaping today, my little H. G. Wells wannabees," he said. "It's really getting to be time for my . . . *medicine*. I've wasted enough time here, thanks to you lot, and I must be getting on—by myself."

With a swiftness Mindy never could have anticipated, Sheriff Corwin reached over and grabbed Jasper by the hair and slammed his head into the side of the wagon. Jasper's body dropped to the wagon floor. "I find physical violence to be extremely underrated. Don't you, Mindy?"

Mindy backed up in the wagon and Minister Hartthorne stepped between her and Corwin. "Leave her alone!"

"You know, I always thought that 'ladies first' rule was lame." He swung at Hartthorne and contacted hard, but the blow barely fazed the brawny minister. Hartthorne grabbed the sheriff around his middle, shoving him into the side of the wagon.

"*Ooof!* I see you're trying to postpone your unconsciousness," Corwin grunted, edging out of Minister Hartthorne's hold.

As the sheriff stood up awkwardly, Mindy grabbed the horse's reins and gave them a flick—just enough to make the cart lurch as Corwin was still regaining his balance.

The sheriff tottered at the edge of the wagon. Mindy took off her heavy leather shoe and clocked him on the head with it.

Sheriff Corwin tumbled out of the wagon, disoriented.

"Hold on, minister!" Mindy said, flicking the reins in earnest now. It was tough with her hands bound in front of her, but from experience Mindy knew that horses responded more to how you said something than to a crack of the reins. "Go, boy!" she said. "Get us out of here!"

Responsive to her direction, the horse took off at a gallop. Corwin didn't stay down for long. He jumped up, shook his head, and charged down the road after them.

"Faster boy, faster," Mindy said to the horse, which immediately boosted its speed.

Sheriff Corwin dropped to a walk as the wagon quickly outdistanced him.

Mindy reigned the horse in. "Good boy," she said softly. "Good boy." She took one last glance back and saw Corwin, off in the distance heading toward town. Several men on horseback appeared on the horizon. The sheriff flagged them down.

Mindy didn't know how badly Jasper was hurt, but she couldn't do much for him with her hands tied as they were in front of her. The best thing to do was to just let the chronolyzer transport them to Jasper's time and get help there. But first she had to deal with Minister Hartthorne.

"You've got to get out of here," Mindy said. "They're going to be coming for us."

"But Jasper is hurt. You cannot travel with him like this."

"I'll take the cart and get him to a doctor. You go the other direction. I'm sure you have friends or family outside of Salem. Stay with them."

"I'm not abandoning you here." His emerald eyes glistened with sincerity.

"I need you to listen to me. If we split up, we all have a better shot at getting away."

"I do not believe I should get away," Minister Hartthorne said. "I have done nothing wrong. When I am tried, the truth will be revealed. God cannot suffer so many good men to be in such an error about this matter."

Off to the side, Mindy heard the clip-clop of horses. The bushes rustled. Someone said, "I think I see the wagon!"

Mindy was out of options. She hated to hurt Jonathan, but she knew what she had to do. Speaking with the voice she reserved for when her sister got her *really* mad, she said, "Minister Hartthorne, you are a naïve and self-righteous man, and if you want to swing on Gallows Hill, you just go ahead and turn yourself in!" Mindy picked up the chronolyzer. "Chronolyzer, I drank the tempose. Transport us to Jasper's home base."

ABOUT TIME, the chronolyzer displayed. I WAS WORRIED I'D BECOME OBSOLETE WAITING FOR YOU. BEGINNING CALCULATIONS . . .

On the floor of the wagon, Jasper stirred. "Mindy, what happened? Where's Andros?"

CALCULATIONS COMPLETE, the chronolyzer typed. EXECUTING TIME-TRAVEL SEQUENCE FOR THREE HUMANS.

"Three?" Mindy said. "Chronolyzer, I didn't mean—"

COMMENCING, the chronolyzer typed.

Epilogue

The world swirled out of focus, and Mindy felt as if a miniature baseball-pitching machine were inside her stomach, bang-dropping balls into the lining. The blackness of time travel smelled like chocolate chip cookies and sulfur. When Mindy opened her eyes, the world was white.

Mindy lay on a chrome exam table, still in her green wool skirt and waistcoat. Cautiously she sat up. Her feet dangled over the side of the table, one of her uncomfortable leather shoes missing.

The blindingly white room was a monochrome *Jetsons*like vision of the future. Computers and a bank of unidentifiable machinery lined one wall. An office area contained a white plastic desk and chair. Mindy seemed to be in some sort of medical station. On the next table over, a very buff, very *naked* Minister Hartthorne blinked awake. "Is this heaven?" he asked. "I'd have thought it would have more clouds."

Jasper blurred past Mindy, slapping a square blue patch on the minister's arm.

Minister Hartthorne passed out again.

"Where am I?" Mindy asked. "And why isn't Minister Hartthorne wearing any clothes?"

"The year is 2512, and you're in a Safe Room in the transportation hub at Time Stream Investigation headquarters."

"And the no-clothes thing?"

"Clothes don't survive time travel."

"But *I've* still got *my* clothes on."

"No, no, no. Those may look like the clothes you were wearing, but you're actually wearing a transparent body stocking that allows the chronolyzer to program period-appropriate clothing onto you." He looked uncomfortable and lowered his voice. "I, ah, actually put it onto you when we came to Salem, while you were still unconscious following the blast of the chronobomb. I figured that would be easier on you than waking up naked. You could just as easily be wearing a Renaissance ball gown or neon spandex from the 1980s, but I had the chronolyzer replicate the period costume you had on to begin with."

"My brain hurts," Mindy said. "I just want to go home."

"Okay," Jasper said, pressing a button on the chronolyzer.

Traveling through time felt like riding the Cyclops on the New York State Fair midway after downing six envelopes of Pop Rocks and guzzling a two-liter of Coke. With a *thud,* Mindy plummeted into a mauve vinyl visitor's chair beside a twenty-first-century hospital bed.

"Jasper Gordon, when I get hold of you, I'm going to take that chronolyzer of yours and shove it up your nose," Mindy muttered.

A musical, lilting male voice came from behind her, sending chills down her spine. "Sure and it might not fit, Mindy."

Mindy turned to glare at him. "You've got to stop chucking me through the space-time continuum without any warning," Mindy said, yanking the Puritan mobcap off her head and fluffing her thick brown hair.

Jasper shrugged, his hazel eyes glittering mischievously. "You said you wanted to go back to your own time."

"Yeah, but not right that very second. Some notice would have been nice."

"I don't have time to hold your hand through every little detail," Jasper said. "I've got Andros to catch."

"Do you think you could at least get rid of this archaic Puritan skirt and blouse before you gallop off in search of Andros again?"

Jasper fiddled with the chronolyzer. Mindy's scratchy wool skirt became faded jeans, and her waistcoat melted into a black and orange Witchcraft Heights High T-shirt. Her favorite pair of black canvas Keds finished off her outfit. "Better?" he asked.

"Yeah, but why'd you zonk me to a hospital instead of my bedroom or something? How am I supposed to get home from here?" She looked around. "And what have you done with Minister Hartthorne?"

"The Holy Man is still on that slab in the future, waiting to be reintroduced into his own time. As for your ride home, your mum will be arriving soon. She'll take you."

"Why would my mom be coming to a hospital?"

Jasper nodded toward the hospital bed that, until now, Mindy hadn't realized was occupied. Mindy's gaze trailed up the too-white linens tucked in around the slight frame of its occupant. The bars surrounded the teenager in the bed like teeth in the gaping maw of an ogre. Mindy forced herself to look at the face. The calm, freckled visage of her fifteen-year-old sister Serena rested on a stiff, chalky white pillow.

"What's wrong with her?" Mindy said.

"To twenty-first-century medical experts, your sister appears to be in a coma."

"But that's not what it is, is it?" Mindy dreaded the answer.

"No, no it's not. Her body is here, but her spirit is in the past."

"Take me to her. We need to get her back. And the others . . ."

"I've got to get back to 2512 to pick up a few things and go search for the other teens Andros sent back in time. Your mom should be here any minute so—"

"How are we going to find my friends?"

"The chronolyzer will transport *me* to the correct general location and time. A body with multiple spirits tends to stand out."

"Stand out as a psycho, you mean."

"They do tend to come off as mentally ill," Jasper conceded. "Once the various spirits begin to wake up in the body, the host displays the symptoms of multiple-personality disorder."

"And when one of those spirits is an alien, it's even tougher to appear normal," Mindy added.

Jasper looked at her. "So what is your point?"

"The weirder people act, the greater risk they're at in the past. Look at what happened to us in Salem Village. We could have hung on Gallows Hill thanks to Andros."

"And?"

"And so I'm going with you."

The young time-cop shook his head. "Negative. Time Stream Investigation policy strictly forbids—"

"I get it," Mindy said. "You're a by-the-book kind of guy. Fine, but you're never going to find my friends without my expertise."

"The twenty-first century is part of my beat," the Time Stream Investigator said. "I've been well-briefed in the era."

"But you don't know as much as I do about the specific teens or what is normal and what isn't for them."

"I can't allow it. My *superiors* would have me permanently reassigned to the Department of Eternal Misfiling."

"But wouldn't your bosses do the happy dance if you found the missing teens quickly?"

"I can't discuss this any further," Jasper said, entering coordinates into the chronolyzer. "Farewell, Mindy Gold."

"Wait! You've got to let me go. I can't just sit next to my sister's hospital bed and wait for you to get around to finding her and sending her back." Mindy dug her nails into her palms. "I'll go crazy. You have to let me help." She felt the tears well up in her eyes.

Suddenly Jasper's eyes glinted. "Right. Okay."

Mindy sniffed. "Okay?"

"Sure." He pushed his curly hair up off of his forehead. "After all, you didn't do half-bad once you got used to the time period, and it *is* your sister we're talking about. I think I'd have a hard time keeping you in the twenty-first century."

"Yup." Mindy gazed at the young Time Stream Investigator. He was smart and loyal and stunningly beautiful, even if he was no bigger than she.

If Jasper were a girl, Mindy would have been jealous of him.

"I suppose you know I'm going to get in big trouble for this, don't you?" Jasper said.

"Once in a while you've got to throw the book out and take a chance on something."

"Or someone."

Heat rose in Mindy's cheeks. "Jasper, I—"

INFRACTIONS LOGGED. TERMINATING AWKWARD MOMENT BY EXECUTING TIME-TRAVEL SEQUENCE, the chronolyzer typed.

The hospital room swirled around Mindy. "I'll be back for you soon, Serena," she said. "I promise."

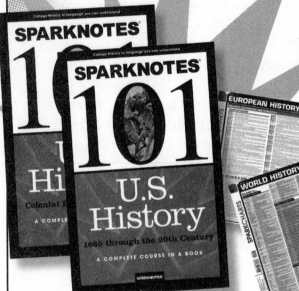